Choose Your own Ever After

HOW TO Get To Rio

First American Edition 2015
Kane Miller, A Division of EDC Publishing

Text copyright © 2014 Julie Fison
Illustration and design copyright © Hardie Grant Egmont 2014
First published in Australia by Hardie Grant Egmont 2014

For information contact:
Kane Miller, A Division of EDC Publishing
P.O. Box 470663
Tulsa, OK 74147-0663
www.kanemiller.com
www.edcpub.com
www.usbornebooksandmore.com

Library of Congress Control Number: 2014941181

Printed and bound in the United States of America
4 5 6 7 8 9 10
ISBN: 978-1-61067-353-2

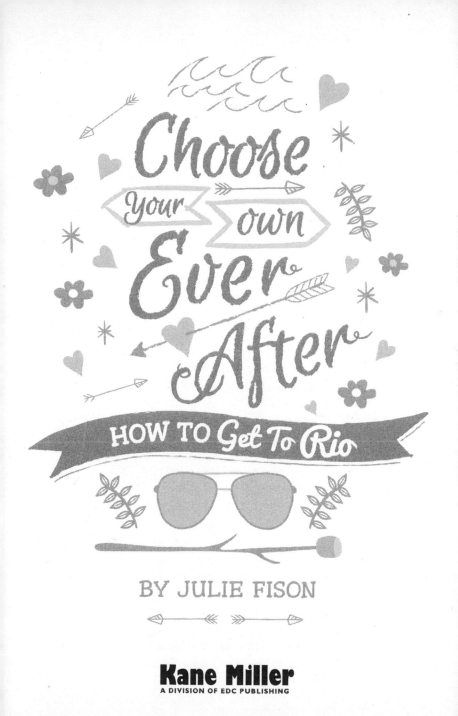

Choose *Your* *own* Ever After

HOW TO *Get To Rio*

BY JULIE FISON

Kane Miller
A DIVISION OF EDC PUBLISHING

Chapter One

"Cam-ping." I said the word like I'd just discovered new vocab. "What, like, in an actual tent?"

Izzy rolled her eyes. "Of course," she said. "So, what do you say?"

"It'll be totally fun," Mia gushed.

I wasn't so sure about that. "But wasn't the last time you went camping the worst week of your lives?" I asked them. "Didn't you say it rained the whole time? And didn't one of your brothers throw up all over your sleeping bags?"

"Come on, Kitty," Izzy said, yanking her math book out of her locker. "What else will you be doing?"

Nothing. That was the problem. It was the last week of school and come next week Mum and Dad would be working, so I'd be stuck at home the entire vacation. That would be fine if I had someone to hang out with. But all my friends were going away, which left me alone with my little sister and her gang of dweebs.

I shrugged. "Okay, I'll come." I knew Mum and Dad would let me go. Izzy and Mia grinned and leaned in for a group hug. "That's provided I survive first period. I haven't done my geography assignment for Blackmore."

"I promise, we'll have *so* much fun," Mia squealed.

"Good luck with your assignment," said Izzy.

I watched them rush off to their homeroom class, their ponytails, wet from water polo practice that morning, dripping down their backs. Izzy and Mia looked like twins from behind. In fact, they looked pretty similar from the front as well. Their homeroom teacher called them both *Mizzy* because he couldn't tell them apart.

I turned back to my locker, frowning. I loved Izzy and Mia to bits. I'd known them since preschool, and they were definitely my best friends. So of course I wanted to go on vacation with them. But camping?

The only tent I'd ever slept in was the fairy princess one that Mum bought when I was three. And that tent was pitched in my room, not in the actual bush.

Mia's and Izzy's families were outdoors addicts and had been camping together heaps of times. But sleeping on the ground was not my idea of fun. Not to mention the spiders, snakes and whatever else that would be trying to get into my sleeping bag with me. Add to that communal bathrooms and long hikes in the bush. Nope. "Fun" was not the word that came to mind. But what choice did I have if I wanted to spend time with my best friends?

I grabbed my geography books out of my locker and spun around, almost crashing straight into Persephone. I got a great big whiff of her perfume and a close-up view of her pearl earring.

I was pretty certain Persephone's vacation plans wouldn't include pitching a tent and fighting for a share of baked beans. It'd be a five-star resort for her, no doubt.

"Hey," I said, smiling.

"Hi, Kitty." Persephone rattled her combination lock and banged open her locker. "Hold on a sec. I'll walk with you."

I waited, feeling slightly confused. Persephone and I weren't exactly friends. We were in the same homeroom class, and sometimes sat together in geography and art, but we never hung out. Then I remembered how recently she'd saved me a seat a couple of times. But still, that wasn't like hanging out. And she'd never walked with me to class before. She always walked with her own friends – the cool group.

I looked around for them. "You're not waiting for –?"

"Nah," Persephone said quickly.

As we headed to class, I was feeling a bit stunned to be walking with one of the coolest girls in our year.

Hello, it's me, Kitty, I felt like saying. *I'm not actually in your group. Your friends are the ones who go on amazing vacations, live in big houses and have real live boyfriends. My house is pretty small, I hardly go anywhere and I'll probably never ever have a boyfriend.*

I didn't say any of that stuff, of course. Instead, I glanced back to check that Izzy and Mia weren't watching me. They didn't think much of the cool group.

I walked along beside Persephone, hoping some of her coolness would rub off on me. She was talking about the geography assignment that was due today that I still hadn't finished. I probably should have been paying attention, but my mind was wandering. *If I were just a fraction as cool as Persephone, I might have a chance with Rio.*

Rio: gorgeous, adorable Rio Sanchez. Totally hot and completely out of my reach. I'd been dreaming about him for months, ever since I first saw him on the bus.

It had been a sticky afternoon and I was standing no more than three feet away from him at the back of the bus. I knew immediately from his uniform that he went to our brother school. I glanced sideways and saw his name on the side of his bag. By the time my eyes had reached his cute tanned face and scruffy dark hair, I was in a trance. Luckily he was too busy laughing with his friends to notice me drooling. Before I knew what was happening I had a vision of our future: walking hand in hand, laughing at each other's jokes, our first kiss.

Then reality had kicked back in. The bus took a sharp corner and, because I was staring at Rio instead of hanging on, I lurched across the aisle. I panicked and grabbed the only thing available – Rio's shirt. He looked down at me with sheer terror in his eyes. He must have thought I was a crazy person. It was so embarrassing. I mumbled an apology and fled the bus at the next stop, which happened to be about a hundred miles from my house.

Since then I'd kept a very safe distance from Rio, but I'd made it my mission to get to know him – without actually talking to him.

Every day when the bus reached his stop, I'd hold my breath, willing him to appear through the front doors. On the days he did, I watched him. He hung out with the sporty guys. They weren't crazy like some of the other boys on the bus, who acted like a bunch of orangutans. Rio and his friends were always laughing.

His brown eyes creased up when he smiled, and he looked so unbelievably cute.

Sometimes, I'd move close enough to hear their conversation. Most of it was about teams I hadn't ever heard of, and players who meant nothing to me. I didn't mind, though. I just liked hearing Rio's voice. He had a bit of an accent. I couldn't place it, but it was totally adorable!

Then one time I saw another side to Rio. He'd gotten on by himself and sat down right in front of me. He had his headphones on and his head was leaning against the window. Out of nowhere a rogue ball came whizzing down the bus towards me. Before I even had a chance to get my hands up to protect myself, Rio snatched it from the air. He tossed it back to its owner and then turned to me.

"You all right?" he'd asked.

I was too tongue-tied to say anything, so I just nodded vigorously.

Rio smiled and got back to his music as if nothing had happened. But when I got off the bus three stops later I was buzzing. *Rio Sanchez had smiled at me!*

I raced home. Then I sat down with my sketch pad and drew Rio's face. I tried to capture his expression. It had been strong, yet caring. And his smile — it was hot enough to melt a glacier. So gorgeous!

I was pretty happy with my sketches. If only talking to Rio were as easy as drawing him.

Pushing my daydreams aside, I remembered where I was — in the corridor walking to class with Persephone. I looked across at her, wondering whether it was makeup or some special face cream that made her skin glow like that. That's when I realized that she was asking me something.

"Kitty?" Persephone said, raising an eyebrow. "Have you done it?"

I had no idea what she was talking about, but tried not to let on that I hadn't been listening. "Ah …"

"Have you done your geo assignment?"

I groaned. "No. I'm going to ask for an extension." I'd obviously spent way too much time daydreaming about Rio and not enough time on my homework.

Persephone smiled. "I've found loads of websites that helped. I can send you the links, if you like."

"That would be amazing!" I was genuinely grateful. "I can't wait till vacation. I'm so sick of school!"

"Me too. It's going to be fun. We're going to Paradise Point," said Persephone. "Does your family go there?"

I shook my head. "Not much."

Just once, actually. Paradise Point was too cool for my family. It was celebrity central. Everyone who was anyone had a place there. Perfect beach, perfect shops and perfect people. Not my family's style at all.

"We've got an apartment right on the beach," Persephone told me.

Of course you do, I thought.

"You should come and stay with us sometime."

I stopped and looked around. Was Persephone still talking to me? Maybe one of her friends had turned up. No. She was looking right at me.

"Stay with you? At Paradise Point?"

Persephone looked like she was sorry she'd asked. "I mean, it's okay if you don't want to."

"No, no. I mean, yes!" I said. "I'd love to."

"Well, I don't know when, but we should definitely organize it!" Persephone cheered. "It's so fun there. Long hot days at the beach, ice cream to die for, *loads* of hot guys, and then hanging out late at night. We'll have to organize it sometime."

"Totes." Now that sounded like my idea of fun.

"Just one condition."

I should have guessed there'd be one. Hanging out with the coolest girl at school in her beach apartment did seem a bit too good to be true.

Persephone looked serious. "You can't ever, *ever*," she paused, "use my nickname."

"Oh, easy," I said, feeling relieved it wasn't some kind of coolness test I had to pass. "I don't even know your nickname."

For a second Persephone looked shy. "My family calls me Percy Pony. My brother started it when he was three, and it stuck."

I smiled. "It's cute."

"Use it and you're dead," she replied, half laughing.

I crossed my heart solemnly. "Promise I'll never use it." I hesitated. "You know what my family nickname is?"

Persephone leaned closer, smiling.

"Kitty-cat."

She giggled. "That's *really* cute."

I screwed up my face. "Maybe when I was six. But now it's just embarrassing, especially when I've got friends over and Mum uses it." I shuddered just thinking about it. Then I had another thought. *Perhaps I shouldn't have just blurted that out to the coolest girl at school.*

But Persephone just shook her head. "Parents are so annoying. I hope mine grow up one day!"

We both laughed. Persephone slipped her arm through mine and we walked into class together.

I was bubbling with excitement. Had I suddenly made a very cool new friend?

Chapter Two

By the time the bell rang for lunch, I realized that something new and super exciting was going on in my life. It seemed too early to call Persephone a friend, but things were definitely changing between us. Little things like her saving me a seat and walking with me to class were small signs. But there were bigger signs, too. She'd invited me to stay with her and she'd even shared her secret nickname. She was breaking the ice between us. We weren't real friends yet and we were still in different groups. But I felt like now I had a chance to really get to know her, and I realized that she wanted to get to know me, too.

Maybe we could hang out one weekend over vacation? Perhaps we could go shopping or to a movie? I'd only be camping for a week. After that Izzy and Mia would be back in the pool. I'd definitely have free time to hang out with Persephone.

It wasn't like I wanted to trade in my besties, but I did like the idea of a new friend. Especially one who had time for fun. Persephone would probably be super busy over the break, but I figured it couldn't hurt to ask.

I waited for her outside the classroom. She finally came out with Tori, her best friend. Tori wasn't as pretty as Persephone, but she stood out in the group because she had confidence, and loads of it.

Tori was the one who started the whole braid trend at school. One day she wore a braid and the next day most of the girls in our year were wearing their hair like that. Except for the water polo girls and me. We wore ponytails. Not that I played water polo. But I did my hair like them because that's who I hung out with.

"Hey there," Persephone said. But before I had a chance to ask her about hanging out, Tori led her away.

Persephone threw her arm in the air dramatically and arched her body backwards, like she was being dragged off to prison. She waved for me to follow. "Want to have lunch with us?" she called out.

I grinned at the idea, but then shook my head. I always had lunch with Izzy and Mia. It wasn't every day that I was invited to have lunch with the cool girls, but I knew it would be uncool to ditch my friends.

Mia and Izzy were at our usual bench. They smiled, but I could hardly meet their eyes. All of a sudden I felt a bit guilty for even considering having lunch with Persephone and the cool girls.

"You okay?" Izzy asked as I sat down. "How did you go with Blackmore?"

"Okay," I said. "Got an extension. Until Thursday."

"How fun, doing assignments in the last week of school," Mia said, rolling her eyes.

"I know," I said with a sigh, "but Persephone said she could give me a bit of help with some websites."

Izzy's face twisted into a grimace. She looked like she'd just sucked a lemon. "*Persesame*?" Izzy intentionally mangled Persephone's name. "Since when are you two besties?"

"We're not," I shot back. "We're just in the same homeroom, so we sit together in class sometimes, that's all." I hesitated. "And, you know, I hang out with her at the bus stop when you two have water polo practice after school. Anyway, she was just trying to help."

Izzy stuffed a piece of nutritious-looking muffin into her mouth. She still had a sour-lemon look on her face when she finished. "I just don't trust her."

"You don't even know her!"

Izzy shrugged. "I know enough." Then she came up with a long list of reasons for not liking Persephone. Most of them were ridiculous. She didn't like her name or the way she wore her hair or the way she talked. But Persephone's main crime, according to Izzy, was being in Tori's group. "They're all stuck-up."

I glared at my half-eaten granola bar. Izzy didn't know anything about Persephone. Maybe some of the girls in her group were stuck-up, but Persephone wasn't. And besides, I didn't need Izzy's permission to be friends with Persephone, or anyone else.

"Persephone's actually really cool," I said. "And she loves The Lads, too."

Mia and Izzy groaned. They couldn't stand The Lads and always complained when I played their songs.

"I don't know," Izzy said slowly. "There's something not right about a girl *that* pretty."

I couldn't believe what I was hearing. "So *that's* why you don't like her? Because she's too pretty?"

Izzy shrugged.

"Izzy, what's that supposed to mean?" Mia demanded. "So you like us because we're *not* pretty?"

Izzy shook her head. "I didn't say —"

Mia cut her off. "Kitty's prettier than Persephone. How come you like Kitty?"

Izzy shrugged again. "Kitty's different. I've known her since forever. I knew her when she wasn't so pretty."

"Hey," I protested.

"Remember that time you came to a party in third grade as a cave girl," Izzy said, giggling, "and you were wearing some old sheepskin thing out of a dog's basket? And your face was covered in charcoal? And your hair was all stiff and covered in leaves, like you'd been sleeping in the backyard for a week?" Izzy started choking on her laughter. "No, Kitty, you were definitely *not* a pretty sight. Your mum sure does have a warped sense of humor."

"True," I said with a laugh. It was always hard to stay angry with Izzy, especially when she had so many embarrassing primary school stories up her sleeve. "What was Mum thinking?"

Mia smiled at both of us. She hated arguments and looked pleased we were friends again. "It's so great we're all going camping together."

"I know!" I beamed, even though I was still nervous about it. "A whole week in a tent. Yeah! It's going to be *beyond* amazing!"

Izzy and Mia exchanged glances. I could tell that I'd laid on the enthusiasm way too thick.

"You're gonna love it," Mia said. "Trust me."

Izzy smiled cheekily. "But you know we'll be roughing it?"

I shrugged. "I can manage without a hair straightener for a week. And I'm not scared of a cold shower."

Izzy laughed. "There won't be showers where we're going. And we'll have to dig our own toilet."

I flinched at the thought of a do-it-yourself toilet — the humiliation of leaving the campsite with a shovel and a roll of toilet paper, not to mention the flies and the smell. Oh, the smell! And what if I accidentally dug up someone else's toilet? Gross!

Mia looked worried. "You okay?" she asked.

I really wanted to erase the bush toilet from my mind. "So, anything else I need to know about this camping trip?"

"You're okay with snakes, aren't you?" Izzy asked.

Izzy knew I was *not* okay with anything that wriggled. Even lizards gave me the creeps. I knew they had legs and didn't actually wriggle, but they were still too close to snakes for my liking.

But I could see how excited my besties were that I was finally going on one of their camping trips. "I'm okay with snakes. As long as they stay outside the tent."

"And you don't mind leeches? There'll probably be a few around at this time of year," Mia said.

Just the idea of one of those slimy blood-sucking worms of evil attaching themselves to my leg made my skin crawl. I used my shoe to brush off an imaginary leech from my ankle.

Izzy giggled, and I laughed, making out it was all a joke. But I knew it wouldn't be so funny when I was actually in the bush. I wasn't sure I was tough enough to handle leeches and snakes. I wanted to spend a week with Izzy and Mia but I didn't want to put up with leeches or go without a shower to do it, and I certainly didn't want to dig my own toilet. I was starting to regret agreeing to go away with them.

"I like your attitude, missy," Izzy said, putting on a coach's voice and giving me a hard pat on the back. "I know you hate leeches. But you won't let them beat you."

Then it occurred to me. Maybe I *could* get out of the trip. "I hope Mum lets me go," I said, sounding unsure.

"Of course you're coming," Mia said. "Mum said that she was calling your mum today."

"Great," I said feebly. I knew Mum would probably say yes. I was doomed.

"It's gonna be so cool," Mia said. "Eating marshmallows around a campfire, staying up all night telling ghost stories. You'll see."

The bell rang for the end of lunch.

"Kitty, don't forget we've got a water polo meeting later. It's tryouts, remember?" Izzy said.

I shook my head. "There's no way I'll make the team."

"You're great. C'mon, give it a try," Mia said.

"Nah, I have to do my assignment." I sighed. "And, anyway, water polo's not really my thing."

I still wasn't sure what "my thing" was. I guess I was still looking.

I was actually okay at sports. But Izzy and Mia were so freakishly good they made everyone else look useless. They were super committed, too. Both of them had made the elite water polo squad at the beginning of the year. Ever since then they hardly ever had any free time. They were always at practice.

That's probably why I liked the idea of spending time with Persephone. Even though she was one of the cool girls, she was quite normal compared to Izzy and Mia. Persephone and I probably had quite a bit in common. It seemed she liked shopping, doing her nails, and going to the beach. Izzy and Mia, on the other hand, thought *camping* was cool. They basically only had one week a term off practice, and they wanted to spend it with snakes and leeches. Who did that?

I headed off to class, wondering how I was going to survive the camping trip. *Why did it have to be camping?*

I gulped. This trip was going to be awful.

Chapter Three

Peering into my underwear drawer on Thursday morning, I asked myself the big question: *Undies with no elastic, or Snow White and the Seven Dwarfs?*

Ever since Mum started her new job, the chances of finding clean underwear any day of the week were slim. All I had were a couple of pairs that should have been thrown out at least three years ago.

Snow White would have to do. Somehow I managed to wriggle into them. Then I threw on my uniform, grabbed my bag, stuffed in my finished geo assignment and raced out the front door.

After handing my assignment in to Miss Blackmore, I saw Persephone at the lockers.

"Looking forward to bridge building?" she asked.

Bridge building? I'd been so busy finishing my assignment that I'd totally forgotten about it. We were going to spend the whole morning working with guys from our brother school, literally building bridges out of craft sticks, in the hope that we'd build "healthy and harmonious relations" with them. That was our teacher's idea, anyway. Really, we'd be spending the morning checking out potential boyfriend material.

As Persephone turned to a mirror inside her locker to apply some strawberry-scented lip gloss, I took the opportunity to rearrange my undies. They were threatening to cut off the blood supply to my legs.

"Coming?" she asked. She looked perfect as usual.

"Ah, no," I said, running my hand through my hair. I could feel my ponytail was lumpy. "I'll catch you up."

"All right, I'll save you a seat."

I ran to the bathroom to fix my hair and rearrange my Snow White undies again. After I raced back to my locker for breath mints, I was really late for the bridge-building session.

I peeked in from the doorway. I saw Persephone at the back of the room with an empty seat beside her. Two boys were at the lab bench with her. I guessed they were our partners. They looked all right from the back, but then most people looked okay from that angle.

Miss Blackmore was up at the front explaining the exercise. Quietly, I slipped into the classroom and took my seat. I smiled at Persephone and tossed my sketch pad on the bench. It was only then that I looked up to acknowledge the two guys that we'd be working with.

I froze.

One of them was Rio.

It was one thing to watch Rio on the bus from a safe distance, but it was a totally different thing to sit opposite him for two hours. What was I going to say?

"Jordan and Rio, meet Kitty," said Persephone.

Rio was looking right at me. My heart started

thumping like I'd just run two laps of the track. When he leaned in towards me, I could feel my cheeks getting hot. I put my head down and stared at the desk, finding a black "Real Madrid" sticker on Rio's folder to study. I guessed it was his favorite team.

"I know you from the bus, right?" he said.

Oh, no! I thought, suddenly looking up from Rio's folder. He might have remembered saving me from the rogue ball, but it was more likely he'd noticed me staring at him practically every afternoon on the bus. He probably thought I was a stalker!

I was choking on the lump in my throat, but I had to play it cool. "You do look kind of familiar," I said, casually. "We catch the same bus, do we?"

Rio gave me a knowing little smile. I wasn't fooling anyone. *How embarrassing.*

I turned my attention to the front to avoid any more questions. Miss Blackmore was still talking about bridges. I wasn't sure exactly what she'd just said, but the whole class was sniggering.

Miss Blackmore waited until everyone was quiet

before she continued. "Do we have an artist who could sketch a bridge design on the whiteboard for us?"

I slid down in my chair to try to make myself invisible. But I could feel her looking straight at me.

"Kitty MacLean, would you grace us with your drawing skills?" she said, holding up the whiteboard marker.

It didn't sound like I had a choice, so I reluctantly scraped my chair out.

Giggling started before I reached the front of the room. By the time I was at the board drawing, everyone was in hysterics.

What exactly is so funny? I wondered as I sketched a bridge on the board. My bridge was a bit wonky. I tried to block out the laughter, and grabbed the board eraser to rub out the wonky lines.

Behind me, I could still hear the class sniggering and giggling and I could feel my cheeks getting red. I quickly drew the lines back in neatly. As I took a couple of steps back to check my picture, there was a huge snorting laugh. I just had to find out what was so funny.

I spun around to face the class, and saw that every single person was staring at my bottom.

I reached around, and that's when I realized: the back of my skirt was tucked into my undies! Snow White and the Seven Dwarfs were waving at the class!

Two guys in the front row were waving back and another one, who looked a lot like Dopey, was whistling "Hi ho, hi ho, it's off to work we go."

Oh. My. God. It was definitely the worst moment of my life. Period. I wished I could disappear into the floor then and there. But I didn't, of course.

Instead, I flicked my skirt free and turned back to the board. I squeezed my eyes shut to block out the world. But there was nowhere to hide. All I could do was take a deep breath and just finish drawing the bridge that the teacher had asked me to draw.

"Very well done, Kitty," Miss Blackmore said kindly. "You can return to your group now."

I slunk back to my seat, with my eyes glued to the floor. I couldn't look at anyone, least of all Rio. I was sure Persephone would never be friendly to me again.

I put my head in my hands, silently cursing Mum for being too busy to do the laundry.

Someone touched my hand and then I heard Persephone whisper, "It's okay." I opened my eyes and glanced at her sideways.

"That was a great bridge you drew. And you've got a cute butt." She looked to Rio and Jordan for support.

I groaned. She might be trying to help, but she was making things worse. Now Rio and Jordan were staring at me.

"Great bridge," Jordan said, grinning.

Rio nodded. "You're really good at drawing."

"Mmm," I mumbled, putting my head back into my hands.

I noted the time and the date. This was it. The end of the world as I knew it.

Chapter Four

For the next two hours my Snow White underwear haunted me. I tried to do my bit. Somehow I managed to design a bridge for our group, but after that it just felt too hard and I left the others to it.

I went back to my sketch pad. I drew a mythical forest filled with owls, wolves and a fire-breathing dragon. I drew myself on a wobbly old bridge, right in the middle of it all, because that's how I felt. I was lost in the middle of a hostile place – high school.

I had to admit Persephone was trying really hard. She asked me at least twenty times if I was all right

And she kept trying to get me back into the group, making up jobs to involve me.

"Kitty, can you put a stick in that tiny gap? It needs your magic touch," she said at one point. Another time there was something that needed gluing with my "magic touch."

It was sweet of her, but I knew she was just doing it because she felt sorry for me. I didn't have a magic touch – a cursed touch was more like it!

"I wish I could draw like that," Rio said, leaning in to look at my picture.

Jordan nodded. "Yeah, bro. Dragons would make a good change from soccer balls. That's all you ever draw, isn't it?"

Rio elbowed his friend. "You're joking, right? You can't even draw a straight line. Maybe Kitty could help you advance to a stick man."

For a second, it felt like I was floating. I loved hearing Rio say my name and I couldn't help smiling at his compliment. But when I looked at my picture I crashed back to earth. The picture was rubbish. That's when I realized Rio was saying nice things because he felt sorry for me. "It's just a doodle," I mumbled.

I sank down in my seat, brooding. Of all the days I could have had my skirt stuck into my underwear, why did it have to be today? Why couldn't it have happened yesterday, when there were no boys at school? Why not this afternoon? Why did it have to happen during the bridge-building session? Why did it have to be in front of Rio? And why, oh, why did I have to be wearing Snow White undies?

At last, the bell sounded, signaling the end of my torture.

I tore my dumb picture out of my sketch pad, scrunched it into a ball and tossed it into the trash can.

Persephone gasped. "But that was really good. Better than the stick bridge."

I glanced at my group's bridge. *What a wobbly jumble of sticks and glue! That bridge wouldn't support an ant,* I thought.

"Nice work," I lied, checking the back of my skirt. Then I rushed off without saying good-bye to anyone.

Peals of laughter followed me. I assumed everyone was laughing at me again. I didn't stop to check.

I had to find Izzy and Mia. At times like these only best friends can help.

"Here she is," shouted Izzy as I ran up. "So, how were the boys? Any cute ones? I can't wait till our session this afternoon. It's —" She stopped when she saw my face.

I could feel the tears welling in my eyes. I grabbed Izzy and Mia and dragged them to the back of the science building. It was the only place where we could talk without the whole school watching.

"I — have just had —" I gulped back my tears, "the *worst* morning — of — my — life."

Mia put her arm around me. "What happened? It's Blackmore, isn't it? She gave you detention? What a total cow!"

As I shook my head, a tear escaped. "Worse."

"Suspended?" Izzy gasped.

I shook my head again. "Worse."

"Expelled?" Mia said, her eyes widening. "*Er-ma-gawd*, Kitty. Your mum's gonna freak!"

"No, no," I said, sniffing.

"Well, you can't get arrested for handing in a bad assignment, so getting expelled is about as bad as it can be," Izzy said, looking confused.

"It's not about my assignment!" I blurted out.

I took a few deep breaths. "It's my undies," I groaned. "I flashed them at the whole class when Blackmore asked me to draw a bridge on the whiteboard!"

For a moment Izzy and Mia just stared at me, saying nothing.

"Not in your bridge-building session?" said Izzy frowning. "Not in front of boys?"

I nodded.

"In front of boys!" Mia's eyes went really wide. "Oh, Kitty!" She gave me a huge cuddle.

"C'mon, Kitty. Maybe it's not the worst thing ever," Izzy said, grabbing my hand. "It can't be as bad as that time you dressed up as a cave girl."

"No," I said firmly, "it's worse than that. And I haven't even told you the most embarrassing bit."

Mia and Izzy leaned in.

"They were Snow White undies!"

Izzy yanked her hand away and covered her mouth. I thought it was because she was shocked. But then she started snorting. She always did that when she was trying not to laugh.

"*Izzy!*" I cried. "I have just been publicly humiliated. I nearly died of embarrassment. I deserve sympathy, not pig noises."

"Sorry," she said, stifling another snort. "At least you weren't wearing super-lacy ones."

Mia giggled. "Or saggy old granny undies."

I guessed they were right. Maybe it could have been worse. It didn't stop me from feeling humiliated, though.

But Izzy wasn't going to let me feel sorry for myself for long. She was just getting warmed up. "Yeah!" she said. "Imagine Tori flashing hers and they're actually saggy granny undies. Imagine she's talking to a bunch of guys at the bus stop and the wind catches her dress. It blows it right over her head, and there she is in her old-lady undies."

"That would be funny." I had to agree.

It was amazing how something embarrassing seemed funny when you pictured it happening to someone else. But even as I giggled I was pretty sure I was destined to be uncool all through high school now.

In high school, everyone was rushing around trying to prove themselves, trying to be the coolest, trying to *be* someone they weren't. I could remember a time when it wasn't all so hard.

"Remember at primary school, everyone hung out together?" I said. "It seemed like everyone was popular."

Maybe I was only remembering the good times, but it really seemed like we were all just one big happy gang back then. There was no cool group, no nerds, or hipsters, or emos, or water polo girls, or whatever.

"What happened?" I asked.

Izzy shrugged. "We swam into a big pond, I guess."

"Well, it's okay for you and Mia. You're fast fish. You'll be fine no matter how big the pond is," I said, staring into the distance. "I'm just a small lost fish, with silly underwear."

Mia gave me another hug and Izzy joined in.

"Hey, Little Fish," Mia said softly, "we've got your back."

I hugged them back. I knew I wasn't as fearless or as fast as Mia and Izzy. I wasn't on the water polo team. And sometimes I felt like they were from a different planet completely, but it was good to know Mia and Izzy would always be there for me – no matter what.

"Camping with you guys is going to be so cool," I told them. And this time I really meant it.

"Except when the boys throw slime at you!" Izzy laughed.

Of course, I thought. Just when I was getting all warm and fuzzy about the idea of camping, Izzy had to spoil the moment.

"Just kidding," Izzy said. "Like you said before, it will be beyond amazing. So have your bags ready early. We're leaving at 7 a.m. on Saturday."

That afternoon, I caught up with Persephone. Actually, she caught up with me. I'd been avoiding her since the

Snow White incident. But at the end of the day, she cornered me at the lockers.

"Hey," she said. "I've been worried about you. This morning must have been awful."

I nodded, surprised how worried she looked and sounded. "Thanks. It really was awful."

Persephone gave me a hug and then grinned. "So, do you want to know what happened after you left?"

"I think I already know," I said with a sigh. "I could hear everyone laughing at me."

"No, no. I mean with that picture you drew."

I frowned. The only picture I drew went in the trash.

"Well, Rio's got it," Persephone continued. "That picture? The girl on the bridge with the big eyes? Rio pulled it out of the trash can, flattened it out and took it with him."

"What?" It didn't make any sense to me. "Why would he do that?"

"He didn't say. But I'm guessing he really liked it …" Persephone gave me a sly smile. "Or maybe he likes the artist who created it."

"You're joking, right?"

Persephone leaned towards me. "Kitty, he was checking you out the whole time!" she whispered. "He was watching you draw. I think you really made an impression."

"Yeah, a bad one!" I groaned.

But Persephone shook her head. "You handled that underwear thing so well. If that were me, I would have been out of there. Actually, I'd still be blubbering in the bathroom right now."

Persephone was so cool and confident. I found it hard to believe what I was hearing.

"Seriously. You were amazing. No wonder Rio likes you," she said. "You're brave. Definitely braver than me."

"I'm not really," I said quietly.

I could feel myself blushing, so I looked away. That's when I spotted Tori watching us, her hand on her hip. Persephone waved at her, but Tori didn't wave back. She just waited a few seconds and then stalked off with some girls from her group.

Persephone didn't seem bothered. "What do you

think of Rio?" she asked, after Tori was gone.

I shrugged. "He's okay, I guess."

"Just okay?" Persephone raised one eyebrow.

I knew she could see right through me. "All right," I confessed, "he's totally cute. I see him on the bus. I've had a thing for him for ages."

Persephone's eyes widened. "Interesting! You know, he's going to Paradise Point with Jordan over vacation. What do you think about coming to Paradise Point with me, and we can hang out with them?"

I honestly had no idea what I thought. I was totally confused. Not just about Rio — who must have thought I was the most clueless girl on earth and surely couldn't be interested in me after this morning's disaster — but also about Persephone. Why did she want me to go to Paradise Point with her after I flashed my undies at the whole class? She must've had a million cooler friends than me who she could invite.

But before I had a chance to work all this out, I heard myself saying, "That sounds like the best idea ever — I'm so keen! I'll just have to ask Mum."

"Yay!" Persephone cheered.

"So when are you going?" I asked.

"On Saturday at nine. So we'll be at Paradise Point by lunchtime. I'll text Jordan and Rio and we can meet up there."

As Persephone chattered away excitedly, I suddenly felt my heart sink.

I'd already made plans to go camping with Izzy and Mia on Saturday. I couldn't let my friends down, but I didn't want to disappoint Persephone either. I had no idea what to do.

Should I go camping with my besties and miss out on the chance to get to know Persephone – and my best shot with Rio? Or should I go to the beach with Persephone and risk falling out with my best friends?

If you think Kitty should go camping with Mia and Izzy, go to page 41.

If you think Kitty should go to Paradise Point with Persephone, go to page 80.

Kitty GOES CAMPING
with *Mia* and *Izzy*

Chapter Five

It was a long drive to the campground, which gave me plenty of time to mull over my decision to go camping.

Izzy and Mia were sitting next to me. They spent most of the drive debating which bush food was more nutritious — plants or insects. They also put a lot of effort into explaining to me which leaves were best to use as toilet paper.

"Watch out for stinging nettles," Mia said.

Izzy moaned. "Made that mistake before. I couldn't sit down for a week!"

They can't be serious, I thought. *Surely we could use toilet paper?*

"Well, I can't wait to build a big campfire and toast marshmallows," I said, trying to steer the conversation to a happier place.

"Oh," said Mia, "about that. There's a total fire ban, so we won't be able to toast any marshmallows."

I sighed. *Why exactly had I agreed to go camping with Izzy and Mia? Maybe I'd been too quick with my decision.*

I'd had to tell Persephone that I couldn't go to Paradise Point after all. She'd been totally cool about it and promised to give me more warning the next time.

I pulled out my phone and shot her a text. She would be just leaving for the beach now.

Don't have too much fun without me. And say hi to Rio!

A reply came back a second later.

Wish you were coming, too. Next time! Where are you staying?

I wondered what Persephone would think of me going camping for vacation. She probably wouldn't be too impressed, so I kept my response vague.

A rural retreat.

Persephone replied: *Sounds cool! Hope it's five star!*

I shot back: *Me too!* ☺

"Who's that?" Mia asked, trying to peer at my phone.

"Mum," I lied, shoving the phone back in my bag. "Checking up on me already."

I knew that at some stage I'd have to tell Mia and Izzy about Persephone's invitation, but not today. I didn't want to start the trip with another fight about how stuck-up Persephone was. And I could just imagine how Izzy would go on and on about me wishing I was having a fancy-pants vacation with my new bestie.

"How much longer?" whined a voice behind me. It was BB, Izzy's youngest brother. He was possibly the most annoying of Izzy's three brothers, though there was stiff competition for that title.

The three boys were wedged in the very back seat of the car with all the camping gear. They'd been having a pillow fight almost the whole trip, with just a few breaks to throw tennis balls at each other. When one hit me in the back of the head it did nothing to improve my opinion of camping.

"We're almost there," Izzy's mum called back to us.

"The Lost World is just up ahead."

Izzy's dad turned the car onto a tiny road that became a dusty dirt track.

The Lost World — how fitting, I thought. I just hoped we'd be able to find our way back again.

"Say good-bye to civilization, kids," said Izzy's dad, grinning.

When the car pulled up, Izzy opened the door, but before she even had a chance to get out, her brothers somersaulted right over us and scrambled out. I got out of the car feeling bruised and slightly sick.

Mia's family was already there. They were busy setting up camp next to us. Her mum and dad were unpacking tents and boxes of food. Her four brothers were supposed to be helping, but they were screaming and chasing each other around the campground.

I stood out of the way and looked around, taking in my home for the next week. Ahead was a cluster of tents and, past them, a row of campers were facing the sea. The Lost World was actually a gorgeous spot — there was a dramatic mountain range behind us and the sparkling blue ocean up ahead. It was almost as lovely as Paradise Point, just without the shops and restaurants.

On the very edges of the campground were a playground, a trampoline and a big pool bordered by palm trees — all very promising signs. And there was something else more amazing. A big brick building that looked like … I walked closer to get a better look.

"Communal showers," I gasped, reading the sign on the building.

By then Mia was grinning madly. "Surprise!"

"You mean, I don't really have to dig my own toilet?" I asked, looking around at Izzy.

She just tossed me a sleeping bag and laughed. I felt like throwing it back at her — right in her laughing face! She and Mia had really gotten me this time. I'd gotten myself completely worked up about this trip for nothing.

"You're really funny, you two," I said, scowling, "telling me I'd have to dig my own toilet."

"Come on, Kitty," Izzy said. "We did it because we love you."

"Funny way to show it," I grumbled.

"No, really," Mia said. "The campground is much better than you thought, isn't it? That's because we said it would be terrible. If we told you how great The Lost World was, you probably would have been disappointed. Sometimes you have to be cruel to be kind."

"Hmm ... great theory," I muttered. But really I was only half angry now. I had to admit that maybe Izzy and Mia had done me a favor. "So what about the campfire situation?" I asked.

"We can definitely do that!" Mia said, pulling a double bag of marshmallows out of her backpack. "There isn't really a fire ban."

"Enough chitchat, ladies," Izzy's father said, passing Izzy a large bag. "The tents won't put themselves up."

Izzy took the tent bag to a flat piece of grass and emptied it onto the ground. I stared at the pile of poles, pegs, ropes and nylon.

We're never going to make a tent out of that, I thought.

But a surprisingly short time later, we were sitting inside a perfectly comfortable structure, admiring our work. We'd pitched our tent, blown up our air mattresses, rolled out our sleeping bags and had the whole place looking cozy. Mia had even found some fresh lavender and tied a few sprigs together to make our tent smell nice.

"Camping is actually pretty cool," I announced, lying on my mattress.

Mia winked at Izzy. "I'd say our idea worked."

I huffed. "Yeah, but it nearly backfired," I told them. "You told me so many horror stories that I nearly bailed on you."

"Really?" asked Mia.

"I'm glad I didn't, though," I said. "It's going to be beyond amazing spending the week here together."

"So you forgive us?" Mia asked.

Before I could answer, yelling started up outside the tent.

We had been left in charge of the boys while the parents went off to the campground office. The boys were supposed to be setting up their tents, but there was no way they were doing that. It sounded like they were having a war out there.

Izzy poked her nose out of the tent. "Stop messing around! Before someone has an accident!"

She had barely gotten the last word out when there was a squeal, followed by the whack of something hitting the side of our tent. Then there was another scream and a loud thud as several boys landed on our tent. A moment later our tent collapsed on top of us.

"You rodents!" Izzy screamed as the three of us fought our way out.

By the time we got out, the boys were long gone. Mia spotted BB climbing a nearby tree. The other boys were scrambling after him.

Izzy gave chase. "You're all *so dead*," she yelled from the bottom of the tree.

BB just laughed. "Can't catch us, ya lazy old Izzy lizard." He fired a big seed pod, which just missed her.

"*Dead*! You hear me?" she screamed and looked up at the seven laughing boys in the branches above us. "I hate you boys. All boys! I hate you all!"

The three of us paced around the tree, shouting

threats until Mia stopped in her tracks.

Mia's face was pale and her mouth dropped open. "That's awkward," she mumbled. "I bet they saw the whole thing."

At first, I thought she was talking about her parents. But when Izzy and I followed Mia's gaze, we saw a group of guys leaning on the pool fence, staring at us.

Izzy ducked behind the tree trunk. "You think they heard me shouting?"

"I'm pretty certain people on the other side of the country heard you," I said. "So, yeah, I'd say they did."

Izzy poked her head out. "Geez, that's a shame. How cute are they? Especially that one in the red shorts."

Mia gave them a wave. One of them waved back halfheartedly. Then they all wandered off.

"I love camping," Mia said dreamily.

"Me too," Izzy sighed.

I was beginning to get why my best friends loved camping so much. It was all about the guys.

Chapter Six

"Izzy, you scared them off with all that 'hating boys' stuff," Mia said bitterly as we sat on the beach watching the waves roll in.

"Or maybe *you* freaked them out by waving," Izzy replied.

In the last hour, we'd done at least ten circuits of the campground, looking for the cute camping guys. We'd checked around the tents and the campers. We'd been in and out of the pool three times and walked to the beach, but there was no sign of the guy in the red shorts or his friends. They'd disappeared completely.

"Blame your brothers," I suggested.

"I always do," Izzy said with a grin.

"Yeah," Mia agreed. "If they hadn't destroyed our tent, we wouldn't have been putting it back up when we could have been talking with the guys. And we'd probably be hanging out with them right now, instead of watching seagulls."

Izzy sighed. "The guy in the red shorts was definitely the cutest."

Mia shook her head. "The one in the blue shirt was hotter." She sighed. "But we're not going to find any of them here."

It was starting to get dark, so we headed back to the campground. I dawdled behind to check my phone. I'd heard it beep with a text earlier, but didn't want to check it in front of the girls. While Izzy and Mia kept debating about which of the missing guys was cuter, I opened a message from Persephone.

How's the rural retreat?

I replied: *Pretty good* ☺

Lucky you. Is it a beautiful villa? Have you got a pool?

I shot back: *Of course!*

I knew that was at least half a lie, but before I had time to worry about it my phone beeped again.

So jealous ☺

At least my next text was totally true: *It's amazing here! Wish you could see it for yourself.*

The reply that came back made my heart jump.

You should be here. Just saw Rio at the beach. He looked sad when I said you weren't coming to PP.

Really? I texted back.

Really!

Even though I was having fun with Izzy and Mia, my heart sank a little. While we were scurrying around a campground after some random boys, Persephone was hanging out with Rio. I didn't care about some guy in red shorts or any of the camping guys. They were nothing compared to Rio.

I looked up to see if I could send another text without Mia and Izzy seeing. They were a safe distance ahead.

Now I'm sad I'm here and not there.

Persephone replied: *Don't be! Enjoy the villa. You can see Rio another time.*

It was easy for Persephone to say. She was the kind of girl who could just stroll up to any guy she wanted and talk to him. It wasn't that easy for me. But I wasn't going to mention that.

Sure, I'll see him when I get back. Loving the villa life!

My phone beeped again.

Where's this amazing rural retreat? I'll have to go there sometime.

I could answer that question truthfully. I figured Persephone would have no idea where this place was.

It's called The Lost World.

Then came an unexpected reply.

OMG! That's right near here. I can probably wave to you from our apartment! But I thought The Lost World was just a campground.

I felt sick in the stomach. Straining my eyes to see in the light of sunset, I looked at my surroundings. The beach, the mountains, the rocky headland. No wonder it all looked so familiar, because it was! My phone beeped again.

What's the address of your villa? I'll come visit!

I stared at the message and wished that I had never started texting Persephone. Now she was going to find out that I was a liar and staying at a campground. I wasn't sure which was worse.

"Kitty," Mia called down from the top of the sand dune, "do you have a boyfriend?"

I jumped at the sound of her voice. "No. Of course not." I quickly shoved my phone into my pocket and raced up the dune.

"Let's see your phone, then," Izzy said, sticking her hand out.

I shook my head. "Just needed to get a few things sorted out. Just boring stuff."

"*Sure*," Mia said with a sly smile. "Is that 'boring stuff' related to Rio, by any chance?"

"I wish."

Izzy and Mia were looking at me suspiciously, but they didn't ask any more questions. I was grateful for that because I had enough problems to deal with. What was I going to do about Persephone? I couldn't let her come to The Lost World. There was no poolside villa to see here.

Maybe I could organize to meet her at Paradise Point, I thought. But that meant explaining the whole story about Persephone's invitation to Izzy and Mia, which I didn't really want to do.

"How far is it to Paradise Point?" I asked when we were almost back at the tent.

"It's on the far side of the bay," Izzy said, pointing. "You can't see it from here, but it's just around the headland. Why?"

"Just wondering."

"Wondering why?" asked Mia.

"Just wondering why you didn't tell me that before," I said, grumpily.

Izzy stared at me hard. "Well, because you didn't ask," she said.

I supposed that was true. I hadn't asked. But now that I knew that Rio was staying on the other side of the bay, I couldn't get him out of my mind. I had to see him. I just needed a bit of time to work out a plan.

Chapter Seven

"Guess what?" Izzy whispered, crawling into the tent. "I saw the guys!"

"Did you talk to them?" Mia asked eagerly, propping herself up on her elbows.

Izzy looked down at her clothes. "Yeah, I really had a great conversation while I was in my pajamas!"

I laughed. "You look totally cute. You should have."

"Nice of you to say so, but no, I didn't talk to them. I did get some intel, though." Izzy paused as she zipped up the tent door. "They were talking about the waterfall. You remember the one, Mia — at the top of the Valley of the Beeches?"

Mia frowned. "Valley of the Leeches more like."

Izzy flopped down on her mattress. "Yeah, well, that's where they're going in the morning. We should go, too."

"Could work," Mia said, thoughtfully. "Sounds like a plan to me."

"Let's go early to be there when they arrive. That way we don't look like we're stalking them," Izzy said, turning to me. "What do you think, Kit? A walk through Valley of the Leeches – I mean Beeches – and a swim at the waterfall?"

"Ha-ha. You're funny," I said, smiling. "You're trying to get me all stressed about leeches and then you'll take me on a hike through a valley full of butterflies or something. Well, you're not getting me this time with that old trick."

Izzy shook her head. "Okay, that does sound like the sort of thing I'd do, but we're not messing around. The valley is actually full of leeches. But those guys are actually even cuter close up, so it'll be worth it."

My smile dropped. "But you know how much I hate leeches."

Izzy nodded. "I'm scared of leeches, too," she said. "Everyone is."

I knew she was just saying that to make me feel better, but it didn't. I put my hands over my face. "I can't."

Mia gently pulled my hands from my face. "C'mon, Kitty. You're the only one who hasn't done something silly in front of those guys. We *need* you."

"C'mon, Kit," Izzy said. "All for one and one for all. We'd do the same for you."

I studied my friends' faces in the flashlight's beam. They were so excited about hanging out at the waterfall with a bunch of cute guys. But if I had to walk through leech territory to help them out, maybe they could do me a favor.

"Okay, here's the deal," I told them. "I will come to the waterfall, if you come to Paradise Point with me."

"But why Paradise Point?" Mia said, looking confused.

"To see Persephone."

"No way!" Izzy said, looking fierce. "I'm not spending my vacation hanging out with *Persesame*."

This was just the reaction I expected.

"Please," I begged. "She knows where Rio's staying. I need her help to find him."

Izzy's face brightened. "So this is all about Rio, then? Why didn't you say so?"

I shrugged. It wasn't actually *all* about Rio, but I knew they'd go along with my plan if I said it was. Mia and Izzy would never understand why I wanted to be friends with Persephone, but they had no issue with going to Paradise Point to find Rio.

"Okay, then," Izzy said with a grin.

Mia nodded, too. "It's a deal. We'll help you find Rio and you can help us find the cute campers!"

It was too hard to group hug in the tent, so we made up an epic handshake to make the deal official. We'd been making up crazy handshakes together for years.

Slap-slap, tap-tap, bump-bump, elbow kiss—elbow kiss.

Izzy clicked her fingers. "It needs one of these!"

"It needs two of those!" Mia said, giggling.

While they worked out the rest of our handshake, I texted Persephone to tell her the news.

She replied a second later.

Beyond excited you're coming to PP! Let's meet for a milkshake. ☺

I bounced around on my mattress to celebrate. I couldn't wait for Izzy and Mia to see that Persephone wasn't stuck-up like the rest of her group – that she was like us, just a tiny bit cooler. Okay, a lot cooler.

I sent off a few more texts to sort out the details of where and when to meet tomorrow afternoon. I figured three o'clock would work. That would give us time to get to the waterfall and back, get changed and make it to Paradise Point. Just as I finished texting Persephone, I noticed that my phone was almost out of charge.

"Where can I charge my phone?" I asked.

Izzy waved her hand towards the back of the tent. "Just over there."

I crawled to the end of my mattress, feeling around. By then Izzy and Mia were giggling.

"There's no power outlet in here, is there?" I groaned.

Mia shook her head, trying not to laugh.

"I can't charge my phone, can I?" I said slowly.

"Because we don't have any power."

"My mum doesn't even let me bring a phone," Mia said.

"Oh great," I sighed, suddenly feeling very vulnerable. I looked at my phone again. It was dead.

At least I'd made plans with Persephone before my phone died. But how was I going to survive the rest of the week? It felt like my right arm had been severed. In fact, that might have been preferable.

"But I can't live without my phone," I whimpered, staring at my precious device. It wasn't the coolest phone around, but I'd saved for a year to buy it and I loved it so much.

Izzy gently took my phone from my hand. She tossed it on top of my bag and smiled. "Now, back to more important things," she said. "So I think the guy in the red shorts is called Sam, or it might be Dan or –"

"I think he looks like a Calvin," Mia said.

"Calvin?" Izzy said, making a face. "How does he look like a Calvin?"

We stayed up late getting our cool handshake right

and talking through our waterfall plans for the next morning.

When Mia and Izzy launched back into their conversation about which camper was cuter, I pulled out my sketch pad and started doodling. At least that didn't need charging.

Before long I'd drawn Rio, looking out to sea. It wasn't my best effort, just a quick sketch. But Izzy and Mia thought it was really cool.

I tore the picture out of my sketch pad and tucked it under my pillow. As I drifted off to sleep, I was sure I could feel Rio's big brown eyes watching me from the other end of the bay.

Chapter Eight

The next morning I woke to the smell of frying bacon. Izzy and Mia were still fast asleep, even though light was streaming into the tent and it was feeling a bit like a sauna. As I lay in bed listening to the sounds of the camp, I realized that we were probably the only ones not up. The boys were shouting about who was going to get the last piece of toast.

I stretched across to check the time, but, of course, my phone was dead. Dead to the world, a bit like my friends.

"Do you girls want breakfast or not?" Izzy's mum called from outside the tent.

Izzy groaned.

"I'll take that as a no," said her mum.

A few moments later, I heard our tent door being unzipped. BB crawled in and flopped down onto Izzy's mattress.

"Buzz off, rodent," Izzy mumbled.

"Get up, ya lazy old lizard! We're going fishing," BB said, bouncing on her mattress. "Dad's got the boat ready."

"Too early," Izzy grumbled, trying to swat her brother without lifting her head.

"No, it's not," BB said. "It's ten."

Izzy sat bolt upright. "What? Ten o'clock! But we were supposed to leave at seven." She flicked her brother with a towel, sending him scurrying out of the tent.

"Guess we'd better get ready, then," I said, and gently shook Mia, who was still asleep.

"In a minute," Mia mumbled and went back to sleep.

It was midday by the time we set off. Our late start meant it was unlikely that we'd beat the cute campers to the waterfall. But Izzy was determined to go anyway. She set a fast pace to the edge of the campground where the track to the Valley of the Beeches began.

Izzy was confident that she remembered the way and led us along a dirt track that went deep into the forest. It was a bit muddy and slippery because it had rained overnight, but it was a beautiful walk. Until we entered leech territory.

No one had to tell me we were now in the Valley of the Leeches. I could feel goose bumps springing up on my arms at the thought of those tiny little blood suckers. Every branch that I brushed past made me jump. Drops of water falling from the trees almost gave me heart failure. When a bird flittered past, I grabbed Mia's arm in panic.

"Chill out," Izzy said. "You're not going to get attacked by a leech with all those clothes on."

Even though it was a hot day, I was wearing a long-sleeved top and had my socks pulled up as high as they could go. I looked like a complete dork, but at least I was protected.

"Maybe we could sing to keep your mind off leeches," Mia suggested. She gave a rousing rendition of our school song. It was so terrible that by the time she reached the chorus I'd forgotten all about leeches, but Izzy had heard enough.

"Quiet. I'm trying to think," she said, frowning. "What are we going to do when we get to the waterfall?"

"But I didn't even get to the best bit," Mia said, looking hurt.

We marched on in silence.

"Well," Izzy said finally, "I say we just act normally. Have a swim and wait for the boys to talk to us."

"That'll never work," Mia said. "How about I pretend I'm drowning and wait for one of them to rescue me?"

Izzy stopped in her tracks. "Don't you dare."

Mia laughed. "As if I'd really do that."

"Let's just be brave," I said. "Give them a wave, sit down and have a chat. How hard can that be?"

Mia raised her eyebrows. "So, how's that strategy working with Rio?"

"Not too well so far," I had to admit.

It had been months now, and I still hadn't managed

to say more than a few words to him. And I was certain that since the Snow White undies incident a few days ago my progress with Rio had reached a standstill. So maybe I wasn't really the best person to be giving advice about being brave.

We'd been walking for ages, and I had eyestrain from watching for leeches, when we heard the faint sound of rushing water and a lot of shouting and hooting.

"It's them!" Izzy whispered suddenly.

"How can you tell?" I whispered. It might have been anyone making that noise.

"I can definitely hear Dan!" Izzy said, cupping a hand to her ear.

"I thought his name was Sam," I said.

Mia sighed. "I hope it's Calvin."

We listened for a few more minutes, trying to work out how many people were at the waterfall. We could definitely hear several guys, but there were other voices, too. There were girls' voices.

As we listened, I looked down and saw a black mark on Izzy's ankle, just above her sock. At first I thought it was just mud, but then I realized – it was a leech! I took in a sharp breath and put my hand over my mouth.

"Izzy," I whispered loudly. "Izzy!"

Izzy glanced down at her ankle and screamed. Not a little girly squeal. A full-throated bellow. Her voice echoed around the valley like she was being murdered.

"Get that thing off me!" she screamed, flailing her arms around wildly.

Mia grabbed Izzy's hands. "It's just a leech. Calm down."

But Izzy didn't calm down. She just kept screaming. "Off, OFF! Get it off!"

I couldn't believe it. Tall, strong Izzy, captain of the water polo team, was hysterical. She really *was* scared of leeches.

I just wanted to turn and run – to get out of that leech-infested rain forest and never come back. But I knew I had to help. Somehow I choked back my fear and bobbed down beside Izzy's ankle. I took a deep breath and then flicked the leech from her leg. Izzy let out one final scream as the leech went flying into the undergrowth.

"You all right?" came a voice from down the track.

I turned to see three guys running towards us, their hair wet and drops of water running down their bare chests. It was like a trio of young forest gods had come to rescue us.

"I'm fine," Izzy squeaked. "A leech." She pointed to her ankle.

The guy in red board shorts (known as Dan, Sam and Calvin) bent down to inspect her leg. "Can't see anything."

"I flicked it off," I said as the two other guys gathered around Izzy.

"Lucky. You must have caught it early, before it really got its fangs in," the blond one said. "They don't call this Valley of the Leeches for nothing."

"You're not wrong there," I said, laughing.

I glanced at Izzy. She seemed to have been struck mute. She stared at the guy in red board shorts with her mouth open. Mia was no better. A smile was fixed on her face, and her eyes were frozen on the blond guy.

"We're just going to the waterfall," I said, trying to

fill the awkward silence.

"Maybe not a good idea if you've got a thing about leeches," the blond guy said. "It's totally infested."

"Oh," I said.

"You're not missing much, though. It's more of a wet dribble than a waterfall."

"Oh, that sucks," I replied.

And then more bad news came sauntering towards us – three stunning girls in bikinis. It was like they were using the rain forest track for a catwalk. I could almost hear Mia's and Izzy's hearts being crushed.

"You girls all right?" one of the model girls asked.

"All good now, thanks," I said. But I wasn't speaking for everyone.

"Oh. My. God," Izzy muttered when the group was out of earshot. "I am in love."

We lagged behind the cute-camper gang on the way back to the campground. The leech and the waterfall were all but forgotten.

"Maybe those girls are just their sisters," Mia said hopefully.

"They could be cousins," Izzy suggested.

Mia nodded. "Pretty likely, really."

I kept quiet. It was clear to me the girls and the cute campers were together, and that they were all about sixteen. Mia and Izzy had no chance with those guys, but I didn't want to burst their bubble. Besides, I had troubles of my own.

We'd been gone a long time and we still had to get back to camp, get changed and get to Paradise Point before three. I didn't want to keep Persephone waiting and with my phone dead there was no way to let her know we were running late. I tried to get Mia and Izzy to walk faster, but it was still taking forever to get back.

It didn't help that the ground was slippery, and that Mia was so distracted looking up ahead at the blond guy she kept tripping over every stone on the track. At one stage she fell over and took me with her. When we finally straggled into the campground I saw a clock outside the kiosk. It was already after three.

"Which way to Paradise Point?" I asked Izzy. We didn't have time to change. We just had to go.

Izzy pointed in the direction of the beach.

"But the guys are going for a swim," Mia said, looking longingly at the pool. She was almost drooling.

"Sorry, no time for cute campers. We'll have to run to Paradise Point," I said, taking off towards the beach. I turned around and saw my friends, where I had left them, gazing at the pool.

"You promised," I shouted at them.

Mia and Izzy spent a few more moments watching the guys, or the pool — I wasn't sure which — and then came shuffling after me. We raced down onto the beach, towards the headland that separated The Lost World from Paradise Point. But then we hit the rocks.

We had to leap from one boulder to another, avoiding the sharp barnacles and finding our way around crevices. It was really slow going.

Izzy started to complain that her ankle was hurting from the leech bite. "Can't we go back? We'll see Persephone another time."

It wasn't like Izzy to run out of energy. She must have been angling to get back to see the campers.

"But we're nearly there," I said, trying to distract her. "Just think about the milkshake at the end of the bay."

"I don't even like milkshakes that much," she grumbled.

"I bet they have great cookies," I said.

"Don't like cookies either."

Now Izzy was just being difficult, so I tried another tactic. "Thanks for coming to Paradise Point with me. I know you don't like Persephone much, but it means a lot to me."

"We're not going so you can see Persephone," Mia reminded me. "We're going to find Rio."

"Yeah, of course," I said, taking a deep breath. "But, um, just one more thing …" I knew the only way to tell them was to say it. "I told Persephone we were staying in a luxury villa … so it would be good if you didn't mention we're camping."

Izzy stopped. "What?"

"I'm not asking you to lie," I said quickly. "Just don't say anything about where we're staying."

Mia frowned. "Are you embarrassed to be camping

with us, Kitty?"

I shook my head. "No. I think Persephone might have just misunderstood something and thinks we're staying in a five-star rural retreat."

Izzy caught up with me. "Sorry, I'm not going to lie to impress some stuck-up girl."

"She's not stuck-up and I'm not asking you to lie – I'm just asking you to avoid the subject." Now I was getting annoyed. "And I don't know why you're so huffy. *You* both lied to me about camping."

Mia jumped across a crevice. "Yeah, that was kind of mean," she admitted. "We took it too far, didn't we?"

"You did," I said, indignantly.

"Hey," Izzy protested. "That was different. We were thinking of you when we said all that stuff about digging your own toilet. You were just thinking of yourself when you lied about camping. That's selfish."

I glared at Izzy. "If I'm so selfish how come I just walked through a leech-infested rain forest for you?" I said. "And saved you from a leech attack?"

"Saved me? That was just –"

Izzy was stopped mid-sentence by a flying blob of jelly. It smacked her right between the eyes. She was looking around wildly, just as something whacked me in the back of the head. Then three more jelly missiles landed on the rocks beside us. I looked at the boulders above us and spied where they were coming from. Izzy's and Mia's brothers were pelting us with jellyfish. They dived behind the rocks, laughing like crazy.

"Get down here, you rodents!" Izzy shouted.

The boys responded with another volley of jellyfish.

"You're dead! Dead! All of you!" Izzy screamed.

We weren't waiting around to find out how many jellyfish the Rodent Tribe had stockpiled. We quickly scrambled off in the direction of Paradise Point, with Izzy hurling nonstop abuse at her brothers as jellyfish rained down on us. We didn't slow down until we reached the beach on the other side of the headland.

Paradise Point was like another country. For a start, there were no boys throwing jellyfish at our heads. Then there was the beach – no slippery rocks, just white sand and lots of people. It was jammed with beautiful girls lounging on their towels and guys in board shorts throwing balls. Kids shrieked as they caught small waves on their boogie boards. The smell of coffee drifted on the breeze, and in among the beachfront shops and restaurants I could see our destination: Shake Shifter.

"I just hope she's still there. It must be nearly four by now," I said, pushing my dirty socks down to my ankles and trying to rearrange my top. "And, remember, we're staying in a luxury resort."

"How could I forget that five-star treatment we've been enjoying," Izzy grumbled.

As we got closer to the Shake Shifter, I was relieved to see Persephone sitting outside, talking to Jordan. Even from a distance, I could see that she didn't look as polished and perfect as usual. Her hair had a messy beach look, which made her look even prettier – if that was possible. I watched her and Jordan for a moment, until someone else caught my eye. I started backing away.

"It's Rio," I said, feeling breathless.

"Cool," Mia said. "That's who you wanted to see."

"Yes, but not now. Not like this!" I looked down at

my top and suddenly realized why it wasn't sitting right: there was a tear down the side. My shorts were muddy and I was in filthy running shoes and grubby socks. It was bad enough meeting Persephone in this state, there was no way I could talk to Rio.

"You look fine," said Mia.

"I look like I just walked out of a *Survivor* episode!" I told her. "What about my hair?" Even without looking I knew it was not cute-messy like Persephone's. It felt like a bird's nest.

"It's not as bad as Mia's," Izzy said, matter-of-factly.

"Hey," Mia frowned. "What's wrong with my hair?" She ran her fingers through it and groaned as a blob of jellyfish fell out. "Oh. Gross."

I gave my hair a shake in case I was also transporting jellyfish. Some seaweed dropped onto the sand. "No way," I said. "I can't meet them looking like this."

Izzy shrugged. "If we bail now, I'm not coming back."

Mia gave me a nudge. "Go on, Kitty. Be brave. You always look cute, even with seaweed in your hair," she said kindly. "But I think you'll have to come clean on the camping. You don't look like you've just walked out of a luxury resort."

I glanced over at the three good-looking people sitting outside Shake Shifter. Could I really face Persephone, Jordan and Rio looking like I'd survived a shipwreck? Would that be brave or just stupid? If I didn't, I might miss my chance with Rio. Should I go and talk to Rio and Persephone, or should I go back to the campground and forget about them until school started again?

If you think Kitty should meet Rio and Persephone, go to page 114.

If you think Kitty should go back to the campground with Mia and Izzy, go to page 137.

Kitty GOES TO PARADISE POINT with Persephone

Chapter Five

The view from Persephone's beach apartment was even more amazing than I could have imagined. From the balcony in her bedroom I felt like I could see everyone on the beach – every guy showing off his abs and every girl showing off her tan. We had front-row seats to everything that was happening at Paradise Point without even leaving the apartment. Of course, we *would* be leaving the apartment, just as soon as Persephone had decided on her bikini. She had ten to choose from.

I, on the other hand, had packed two, and had discovered right after I arrived that one didn't actually fit anymore, so that left me with an embarrassingly small number of choices. My blue bikini was it. I had liked it when I packed it, but now, beside Persephone's selection, it looked hopelessly last season.

While Persephone tried on her sixth bikini, I took in the view, trying to spot a celebrity. There had to be one out there. Paradise Point was a magnet for them. My eyes roamed the busy beach, from the point all the way to the headland at the other end of the bay.

"Why's the beach so packed here, and then, past that headland, there's no one?" I asked.

"That's a national park," Persephone called. "You can't see it from here, but there's a campground called The Lost World on the other side of the headland."

Hearing the word "camp" immediately made me feel guilty. I'd called Mia yesterday afternoon and told her I'd sprained my ankle and wasn't able to go with them. It was a complete lie, but I thought it was the only thing to do. I'd agonized over it for a bit. It wasn't like I made a habit of dropping my friends when I got a better offer. But I'd been really stressed about camping, and Persephone had provided me with a perfect excuse not to go. Of course, I couldn't tell Izzy and Mia that. I decided it was kinder just to lie and make sure I kept off Facebook, Instagram and everywhere else, so Izzy and Mia didn't find out the truth.

"How do I look?" Persephone asked, doing a twirl in a cute floral bikini.

"Amazing," I said, completely truthfully.

"What about from behind?"

"The same – perfect." I would have lied if I had to, but I didn't need to. Persephone really was perfect.

She frowned. "What about my fat butt?"

"Who says you've got a fat butt?"

Persephone waved her thumb at her brother's bedroom. George was the male version of Persephone: smooth skin, great hair and a perfect body. He was actually impossibly gorgeous. But he totally knew it.

"So you're going to take the word of your dumb brother over mine?"

Persephone grinned. "All right, let's go. Should we head straight to the beach or check out the shops first?"

"Well, I could do with a new bikini," I said.

She clapped her hands. "Great! Shopping it is!"

Persephone led the way.

"It's a little pricey," she said as we walked down the beachfront, "but totally worth it. This shop has what everyone else at school will be wearing next season."

I followed her inside a tiny busy shop, full of color, music and a lot of very pretty girls who looked just like Persephone.

"It's not normally this packed," she said.

And then we saw why. The sign above the cash register read: *50% off beachwear.*

"Cool!" I said, and headed straight for the racks. I decided to work methodically, from one end of the shop to the other. A few minutes later, I had found a couple of bikinis I liked, but was struggling to find them in my size.

"What do you think of these?" asked Persephone. She had an armful of bikinis and flashed them at me, one by one.

"Wow! I love them all! They're gorgeous," I said. "They'll look great on you."

"Not for me, silly," Persephone said, shaking her head. "I chose them for you."

I checked the sizes. They were all my size. I had no idea how Persephone could guess my size and taste so perfectly. "You should be my personal stylist," I told her on the way to the dressing room.

The line for the dressing room was halfway out of the shop. "There's no way I'm waiting in that line," I said. "Let's come back when it's quieter."

"But there'll be nothing left," Persephone said.

I looked around at the way girls were grabbing things off the racks. Persephone was right. I had to act now. I groaned and joined the mega line.

"You'd look cute in any of these," Persephone said, pulling a purple bikini top from the pile in my arms and holding it up against me. "You know, I have a pretty good eye for sizes. These will fit."

"Okay," I said. Anything to get out of that line. "But which ones should I get? I love them all."

"Get two, then," Persephone said with a cheeky grin. "They're half price."

"I forgot about that," I said. "Thank you, personal stylist!" I looked through the bikinis again, but still couldn't make a choice.

"I'll get them all," I announced and headed straight to the register. I quickly added up the prices in my head. I knew my allowance wouldn't quite cover all of it, but if I dipped into the "emergencies only" money, which Mum had tucked into my wallet, I could afford everything.

"Five bikinis?" Persephone said, raising her eyebrows. "My mum would totally freak if I came home with that many from one shopping trip."

I shrugged. "Mum gave me some spending money, so I might as well spend it. And everything's on sale, so I'm basically saving money."

"I guess, if you have enough money for all of them," Persephone said with a shrug.

"I'll have to dip into my 'emergencies only' stash," I explained. "But carrying around money for emergencies is basically just asking for some kind of accident. Right?"

I was surprised how serious Persephone looked. "But what if you have an actual emergency?"

In that moment, I couldn't think of any emergency that was worse than being at Paradise Point without a choice of bikinis. Surely Mum would understand that!

But I did feel a little guilty when I came out of the shop with a bagful of new bikinis. I'd blown my allowance and put a large hole in my emergencies-only fund. But at least now I was ready for Paradise Point!

Chapter Six

"So what do you think of Paradise Point?" Persephone asked as we spread our towels on the white sand.

"I love it. Who wouldn't?"

"Tori," Persephone replied. "She thinks it's boring."

I didn't say anything. It made me feel uncomfortable to hear Tori's name thrown into the conversation. Ever since we'd arrived at Paradise Point, I'd secretly been wondering why Persephone had invited me and not her best friend, Tori. But now I knew why Tori wasn't here.

"Why does she think it's boring?" I asked.

Persephone shrugged. "That's just Tori. It's just what she's like."

I didn't really know what to say to that. "Let's go for a swim," I suggested.

We waded out into the sea, squealing as the cold waves hit our legs. Suddenly, I realized I didn't know the correct protocol for swimming with one of the cool girls. I imagined that Persephone might want to keep her hair dry and perfect.

But she surprised me by diving underwater. I dived under, too. We splashed around in the shallows, getting warm, and then swam way out beyond the small breakers. The water was surprisingly calm and still that far out.

I was quickly realizing that Persephone was a bit of a fish in the water, just like Mia and Izzy. Well, maybe not quite as good as them. She took a breath and dived underwater. I ducked under, too, and peered at her blurry face, her hair swishing all over it. She made a noise and some bubbles, but I had no clue what she was on about.

"So what did I say?" she said, when we came up for air.

"Ah," I said. "No idea."

"Don't you know Mermaid Speak?" Persephone said, feigning surprise. "The key to it is talking slowly and deliberately, and listening with your eyes and your heart, not just your ears. Let's go again and see if you know what I'm saying. It's a rhyme." She ducked under the water again, and I followed.

"OOo ooo ah ee ah ow ow ooo," I said, when we both came up.

Persephone giggled. "But it's so easy. How come you didn't get it?" she teased. "I said: 'Roses are red, violets are blue, Rio is cute and so are you!'"

"Aw, sweet," I said, smiling. "All right, my turn! It's a limerick. And you're in it." I dived underwater. I bubbled away through the first two lines before I had to come up for air.

Persephone popped up and recited exactly what I'd said. "There once was a girl called Persephone, who liked to eat lots of sesame."

"No way!" I said. "How did you get that?"

"C'mon, Kitty," she said. "There's not a lot that

rhymes with Persephone."

"True," I said, and ducked underwater to finish the limerick. It was quite long and took me several times.

Persephone asked me to repeat the last line a few times. When she finally came up from under the water, she said the limerick almost word for word. "There once was a girl called Persephone, who liked to eat lots of sesame. Along Jordan came, who could say her name, and together they lived ever after so happily."

I couldn't believe it. "How did you get so good at doing that?"

"Years of practice with my cousin," Persephone said. "She's deaf. She has to listen with her heart and her eyes."

"So is she really good at lip-reading underwater?" I asked.

"The best. Maybe she's a mermaid," Persephone giggled and splashed me. "Come on. Race you to shore!"

When we got back to our towels, there was a text waiting for Persephone. She read it aloud.

Hey P. Are you and Kitty at the beach yet? Rio and I are here. When do you want to meet up? J xx

"Oh, and there are two kisses. How cute!" she said, holding the phone to her chest. "So, what do you think? You want to find the guys now?"

"What, like, right now?" I asked. I felt a buzz of excitement at the thought of seeing Rio. It soon turned to panic, though, when I remembered what had happened the last time I saw him. I'd never be ready to face Rio after the Snow White undies incident.

"Uh-huh. Right now," Persephone replied.

"But I won't know what to do," I blurted out. "I won't have anything to say."

Persephone frowned. "Of course you will. Don't be such a worrywart!"

I shook my head. "But I'm not like you. I can't just talk to guys. My tongue will stop working or something. I'm just not cool like you are."

"Well, you look pretty cool to me," Persephone said smiling. "And you act it, too."

I smiled, coyly. "Really? You think so?"

Persephone nodded. "Totes. You rock. You're just a bit shy, that's all."

Was it really possible that I was cool? I looked down at my new bikini. It was definitely cool! Maybe with my new bikini, and Persephone with me, I could face Rio.

"All right, let's meet them. But maybe not right now," I said. "Can we meet them later?"

Persephone smiled. "Of course, silly." She texted Jordan back with a time and a place to meet later that afternoon.

"So what's the story with you and Jordan?" I asked.

"No story yet," Persephone said, giving me a cheeky grin. "But I'm pretty sure there'll be one by the end of vacation."

"How long have you known him?"

"I met him about five minutes before you did."

"What?" I said. "You met him at the bridge-building session?"

"Uh-huh," she said, lying back on her towel.

I found that hard to believe. She and Jordan had seemed so comfortable working together in class that I assumed they'd known each other forever.

"How do you do that?" I asked. "Talk to cute guys without getting nervous?"

Persephone felt around for her sunglasses and put them on. "I've got an older brother. That probably makes it easier for me to talk to guys. Practice on George if you like."

I laughed. "I'd prefer to start practicing on a teddy bear. No offense, but George is kind of arrogant," I said before I could stop myself.

Persephone just laughed. "Kind of! His head's so big he has to duck to get through doorways."

"I guess it's all part of the territory when you're a chick magnet."

Persephone lifted her sunglasses and eyed me suspiciously.

"I don't mean that *I* think he's a chick magnet," I said quickly. "I mean *he* obviously thinks he is. You know what I mean."

Persephone nodded, but I could feel a bit of tension in the air.

"Anyway, enough about George," I said. "I want to talk about Rio. Do you think he likes me?"

Persephone's face relaxed again. "Of course! Who wouldn't?"

I shrugged.

"Hey, stop over-thinking everything. You look super cute in your new bikini," Persephone said, poking me with her toe. "Don't look now, but there are a couple of guys over there who can't take their eyes off you."

She sat up and pointed down the beach at a couple of boys kicking a ball to each other.

"But they're about ten years old," I complained.

Persephone cracked up laughing. "So fussy!" she said. "But seriously, just be yourself and Rio will definitely like you."

"Sure," I said. But that was easier to say than do.

"So what do you ..." Persephone trailed off.

I followed her gaze to two guys near the headland, coming out of the surf. Not the ten-year-olds. These guys were definitely older. *Rio and Jordan?* I suddenly felt butterflies in my tummy.

"Is that who I think it is?" she asked. "C'mon, let's get a closer look."

"Really? Do we have to?" I asked, but Persephone pulled me to my feet.

"I think it is. I think it is," she muttered as we got closer.

But I was more convinced that it wasn't. "It's not Rio and Jordan. Unless they've grown their hair."

"No," said Persephone, "not *them*. It's ..." She glanced around to make sure no one was listening. "The Lads."

"No way!" I squealed.

Persephone put her finger to her lips. "Shh! You'll let the whole beach know. If we're quiet we can keep them all to ourselves."

"What? We're going to talk to them?"

Persephone smiled. "No. Grab your phone. I have a plan."

I shook my head in disbelief. *No way.*

Chapter Seven

My heart was pounding like crazy as we walked towards the two guys. Now that we could see them clearly, there was no mistaking Kes and Pit. Those cute faces, those cool haircuts – who else could they be but The Lads? They were standing right there in front of me, drying themselves off with their towels.

Kes, with his blue eyes and long hair, was the one all the girls loved. But Pit was the one I liked. His smile could melt solid rock. He was probably going to burn a hole right through me if he looked in my direction.

I had never expected to see The Lads at Paradise Point. Maybe a half-famous chef or perhaps a few reality-TV stars, but not these guys. Not The Lads! This really was beyond amazing.

"Let me do the talking," Persephone whispered as we approached. "And remember, play it cool."

That was about the hardest thing she could have asked me to do. My legs had gone to jelly and my tongue felt numb. I hoped Persephone *would* do the talking, because I had no idea what might come out of my mouth if I opened it.

I loved The Lads so much. I had every song that they'd ever recorded and knew all their lyrics. Before Rio came on the scene, I'd kissed my poster of Pit so many times I'd worn a hole in it. I'd even decided where Pit and I would get married. We'd have a Pacific Island wedding. I'd arrive for the ceremony in a dug-out canoe, there'd be frangipani flowers sprinkled across the lagoon and my chiffon dress would ripple in the breeze while Pit waited in a white tux on the shore.

These days, it was Rio I dreamed of in the white tux. But, as I looked at Pit, I was totally in awe. I drifted towards the two guys in a trance. I was in such a daze that I didn't notice Persephone had stopped walking until I bumped into her.

"Wow! Did you see that?" Persephone said, pointing out into the sea. "Look out there. I definitely saw something."

I frowned. *What could she see that was more interesting than Kes and Pit?* The only possibility was Blake and Curt, the other half of the band. Had she spotted them surfing?

"Yeah, I think I can see them," I whispered. "Out past the break."

Persephone frowned and shook her head. "I think I can see a fin," she continued, loud enough for Kes and Pit to hear. Then she gave me a wink.

It took me a moment to catch on. *Oh, right.*

"I think I saw it, too!" I cried, a bit louder than I had intended. "A fin, a fin!"

If Persephone's plan worked, Kes and Pit would be on their feet, scanning the waves for a shark. With any luck they'd rush to the water's edge and ask us what was going on. I sneaked a peek over my shoulder to find out.

Kes and Pit weren't rushing to do anything. They were lying on their towels with their headphones and sunglasses on. They hadn't even noticed us!

A small girl with a bucket wandered over and stood beside Persephone. "Is it a shark?" she asked.

"Don't worry," Persephone told her. "It's nothing."

"Shark!" the girl screamed. "It's a shark!"

"No, no," Persephone said, trying to calm her. "It's just the waves."

But the girl ran back to her family, squealing.

Persephone gave them a wave. "False alarm," she called out.

I glanced over at Kes and Pit. They still hadn't noticed us.

"New plan," Persephone whispered. "Follow me."

She took a deep breath, fluffed up her hair, adjusted her bikini and marched straight towards Kes and Pit. I tried to do the same, but I was basically hyperventilating and all I managed to do was get my sunglasses caught in my hair. So I put them on top of my head, hoping to untangle them from my hair later.

"Excuse me," said Persephone when she was almost standing on top of Kes. Still there was no reaction. "Excuse me, please," she shouted, leaning right over his face.

Kes sat bolt upright. "What? What?" He pulled out his headphones.

Persephone smiled. "I was just wondering –"

"Sorry, babes," Pit interrupted. He sat up and pulled his headphones from his ears. "We're trying to have a vacation here."

I almost started choking as he said the words. Pit was talking to me. I didn't care what he was actually saying. I was hopelessly starstruck.

Persephone cleared her throat. "Sorry, not trying to spoil your vacation. Just wondering if you know the way to The Lost World."

"Oh," Pit said, lying back on his towel. "I thought you wanted an autograph."

Persephone laughed. "Why?" she said, lifting her sunglasses. "Are you famous?"

My heart skipped a beat. What was Persephone

saying? This was Pit and Kes she was talking to, not some schoolboys on the beach. These guys were in a world-famous band.

Pit and Kes looked at each other and scoffed. Kes pushed his sunglasses into his hair. Pit did the same.

"Still don't know who we are?" Kes asked, smirking.

Following Persephone's lead I leaned in close, took a good look at Pit and shook my head. "You look a bit like my cousin Mikey," I said.

Kes laughed and pointed at Pit. "Hey, cousin Mikey."

Pit gave Kes a shove and then turned to me. "You really have no idea who we are?"

I shook my head. "Not trying to be rude," I said, "but I just can't place you."

Pit frowned. "Maybe this will help."

He looked directly at me and started singing the chorus from their smash hit. "Crazy girl, you make me crazy, girl. Girl-crazy, crazy girl. Crazy, crazy, crazy. Whoa!"

Pit hadn't even gotten to the third word when I felt my knees buckling. I dropped on the sand in front of him, my lips mouthing the lyrics. I couldn't wait to tell everyone that Pit had sung me a song!

"I guess you worked out who we are, then?" Pit said, smiling.

I nodded. There was no playing innocent now.

"You had me there for a second, babes," Kes said, looking from me to Persephone. "You know, you're actually pretty cool, for insane stalker schoolgirls."

I couldn't help smiling. It looked like Persephone's coolness was rubbing off on me and we'd only been at Paradise Point for a couple of hours. Maybe by the end of the week I'd be as cool as her.

"Hey, what about a photo?" I said, pulling out my phone. I waited until Persephone shuffled between Pit and Kes. "Beautiful." But just as I took the photo, Kes crossed his eyes. I frowned. "One more, a nice one, this time."

Again, Kes was all smiles until the last moment, when he screwed up his face and pretended he had buck teeth. Then Pit got in on the act and started doing bunny ears behind Persephone. It might have been funny the first time, but by the time I'd taken twelve silly photos, I was getting a bit annoyed.

I deleted the pictures and handed my phone to Kes. "Can you take a nice photo?" I asked. I thought if I split the guys up, things might work out better.

Pit stood between Persephone and me, while Kes snapped away. But when I looked back at the pics, they were just shots of the sand, aside from one picture of us – a terrible one of half of Pit and me. Persephone wasn't even in it.

Kes laughed. "Here, let me have another go."

Persephone handed over her phone this time, and we posed again. Kes set it all up perfectly. For a moment it looked like we were going to get a cool photo, but then he shoved Persephone's phone under his arm and took a picture of his armpit.

"Hey!" Persephone shouted, reaching for her phone.

Kes jumped to his feet and danced away from her, taking more random shots as he went. Then he took a video of Pit picking his nose.

"That's one for the family movie night!" Pit laughed.

"Really?" Persephone said, scowling. She held out

her hand for the phone and Kes dropped it in the sand. Then he and Pit grabbed their towels.

"Hey, great meeting you two," Pit said. "We should do this again." They both laughed and then Pit winked at us. "Catch ya."

We watched them take off across the sand and disappear into a luxury beachfront apartment building.

"Well, that was … interesting," Persephone said, picking up her phone from the sand and shaking it. "Oh, no! My phone's, like, totally full of sand!"

"But what about the photos?" I said.

"They're mostly of Kes's armpit." Persephone groaned, as we looked through them.

Just thinking about how much I'd worshipped The Lads made me feel sick. "That's why they're going straight on Instagram," I said, fiercely, "and we'll upload the nose-picking video to YouTube – so everyone can see how arrogant they are."

We wandered off up the beach, talking through our revenge plan.

Chapter Eight

"Oh, look, we're nearly at The Lost World," Persephone said, pointing to the far end of the headland. "I didn't realize we'd walked so far."

It certainly felt like we'd walked a long way. I sat down on a boulder to take a break. My legs were killing me from jumping over crevices, but we'd been so busy talking I hadn't noticed the pain until now. "I'm dying."

Persephone slumped down beside me. "Me, too. All that scheming sure takes it out of a girl."

I smiled. We'd been hatching our revenge plot since Kes and Pit left us on the beach. We'd posted the details of their beach apartment on one of their fan pages. Pretty soon there'd be a swarm of screaming girls descending on them. No chance of a quiet vacation, then!

We'd also come up with a shortlist of fun things to do with Rio and Jordan over vacation. We decided on a stand-up paddleboard lesson, water-skiing on the lake, trying out the new sushi-train restaurant and visiting every ice cream shop on the beachfront. There were seven to get through – one for every day of our trip!

"I'm so glad you came," Persephone said. "It's only the first day, and already it's the best vacation ever. Well, aside from Kes throwing my phone in the sand."

"But it was Kes! From The Lads!" I said. "That's still pretty amazing."

"Kitty, did you see the photos of his armpit? Trust me, those guys are total idiots."

She was totally right. I was still acting like a groupie. Famous or not, Kes and Pit had acted like complete idiots. But it didn't stop me feeling disappointed that they had turned out to be so lame.

"Losers," I hissed angrily.

"Totes. Major losers. But I'm glad we got to find that out," Persephone said, laughing. "It's cool hanging out with you. When I come to Paradise Point with Tori we hardly leave the apartment. You think *I* take ages to get ready. She takes forever."

I felt uneasy hearing this. Persephone would probably feel guilty later about dissing her best friend.

"With Tori, it's practically lunchtime by the time we get to the beach," she continued, "if we even get to the beach at all."

"Tori doesn't like the beach?"

Persephone shrugged. "She used to. She used to be a laugh, as well. She's witty. And she's really clever. But, now, she just takes everything so seriously. The way she looks, the way other people look. And if she likes a guy, wow, that's like a military operation for her. She is all about planning, detail and precision."

I made a face. "Sounds scary."

"Don't get me wrong," Persephone added quickly, "she's seriously cool. Her mum's some big company boss. Tori's been everywhere and done everything. But, man, she knows how to play the popularity game — favors, put-downs, even lies."

I didn't really know what to say to all this. "So, where is she now?" I asked.

Persephone studied her hands. "At home."

"She didn't want to come to Paradise Point?"

"I didn't ask her," Persephone said.

"Why?" I asked. "Because she'd be bored?"

Persephone was silent for a moment. "This is probably going to sound really bad, but I'm just a bit sick of her. I'm tired of stressing about what I'm wearing all the time. And Tori's got a major crush on my brother. I try to laugh it off, but it gets annoying after a while." Persephone paused and looked at me. "I just wanted to spend time with someone fun for a change. Does that make me selfish?"

I laughed. "No. It makes you normal."

I watched the sea for a bit, processing the idea that Persephone preferred to hang out with me rather than Tori. Tori was so glossy and perfect. I was just average and not perfect at all, but Persephone thought that made me fun. I'd never thought of myself like that before.

It seemed like the right time for my own confession. "I was meant to go camping with Mia and Izzy, but I decided to come here with you because I'd prefer eating ice cream and swimming at the beach to eating burned sausages and digging my own toilet. Does that make me selfish?"

Persephone smiled. "No. It actually sounds pretty normal to me."

"I really like Izzy and Mia. They're amazing and really great friends. But sometimes I feel …" I paused, searching for the right words, "a bit out of place. They're so similar to each other, and that makes me feel different."

Persephone nodded. "I totally get that. Everyone in my group just wants to be like Tori. I seem to be the only one who wants to be a whole separate person. I'm actually a bit sick of all of them. It's much more fun hanging out with you." Persephone looked at me, expectantly, like she was waiting for me to say something meaningful.

But I wasn't quite sure what to tell her. *Surely she*

doesn't want to know that other people think her friends are stuck-up? And then something came to me.

"Why don't you forget about Tori, and hang out with us?"

I could tell by the way Persephone's face lit up that I'd said the right thing. "Really? You think I could?" Then her face dropped. "But I don't play water polo."

"That'll make two of us," I said, grinning.

Persephone's face brightened into a big relieved smile. "Do you think Izzy and Mia will like me?"

I gave her a hug. "Of course they will."

It was settled. Persephone would join our group when we got back to school. I'd just need a bit of time to work on Izzy and Mia to change their minds about her being stuck-up. Once Izzy had an idea in her head she was very determined to stick to it. Her determination made her great at sports, but it also meant she was a bit on the inflexible side. I was confident, though. When they got to know Persephone, they'd see she wasn't like Tori and the rest of her group. Persephone *was* very cool, but she was also really fun.

"Thanks, Kitty," Persephone said. "You're a real friend."

I got to my feet and pulled Persephone up. "Should we head back?"

She nodded. Then something behind me caught her eye. I turned to see two girls coming towards us. For a moment, I thought it was Mia and Izzy. But, of course, it couldn't be. They were camping in some flyblown, remote corner of the country, digging their own toilets and fighting off snakes and leeches.

Then the two girls waved. My heart sank. It *was* Mia and Izzy!

My brain started spinning. I was trying to remember exactly what I'd told them, searching for my excuse for not going camping. *Oh, man! I told them I'd sprained my ankle.*

"Hey. What a surprise seeing you two here," Izzy said, stopping in front of us. Izzy was *not* smiling.

I knew I was in big trouble.

"How's that sprained ankle, Kitty?" she asked. "I'm surprised you made it over all those rocks with an injury like that."

Mia, Izzy and Persephone all stared at me. I knew everyone was waiting for my answer. I had about five seconds to work out what to say.

Should I just tell the truth? Or should I try to get away with the lie about my ankle?

If you think Kitty should tell Mia and Izzy the truth, go to page 157.

If you think Kitty should carry on with her lie about her ankle, go to page 195.

Kitty GOES TO MEET
Rio and Persephone

Chapter Nine

"Hey! I'm glad you made it!" said Persephone, getting up to meet me, Izzy and Mia. She reached out to give me a hug and then seemed to change her mind, and gave my hand a squeeze instead.

"Sorry, my phone died and we got a bit lost getting here," I said, smiling. "Guess that's why they call it The Lost World."

I could hear Izzy groaning at my dumb joke, but Persephone laughed. "Did you see who I found?" she whispered in my ear.

I nodded, glancing at Rio, who was standing outside the cafe with Jordan. Rio had his eyes on me, but he looked more shocked than excited about my arrival. I gave him and Jordan a smile, and introduced them to Izzy and Mia. Then we all stood outside Shake Shifter looking at each other in awkward silence.

"All right," Persephone said finally. "Who's up for a milkshake?"

"Me!" I said, way too enthusiastically.

I felt around for my wallet and then remembered I didn't even have pockets, let alone a wallet or money. I had been planning to change my shorts and get my wallet after our hike. But, of course, that hadn't happened. I had come to Paradise Point with nothing at all. I looked at Izzy and Mia, hoping they had some cash on them.

"Got any money?" I mouthed as discreetly as possible. Izzy shook her head and Mia rummaged around in her pockets but came up with nothing.

Persephone, Rio and Jordan had obviously noticed. Persephone pulled some money from her wallet. "My treat!"

"I'm going to have another swim," said Jordan.

"Me too," said Rio. "Gotta work off the last shake before having another."

I looked questioningly at Izzy and Mia. They shrugged.

"What are you having, Kitty?" Persephone called, heading inside.

We followed Persephone into Shake Shifter. It seemed better to let her buy us a milkshake than pretend we'd suddenly lost our thirst. And to be honest, I was dying for a drink.

We hadn't eaten since breakfast, and the rain forest walk and the climb over the rocks at the headland had left me totally dehydrated.

"Thanks, Persephone," I slurped down my mango smoothie as we sat on the beach watching the guys in the surf. "I really needed this."

"Least I can do for dragging you away from your rural retreat," she said. "It sounds amazing!"

Mia just smirked. But Izzy laughed – way too loudly. "Quite unreal," she said.

Persephone looked confused. I had hoped to avoid

the whole accommodation topic, but it looked like I was going to have to explain sooner rather than later.

"Actually, I was just joking about —" I began.

"Great," came a voice from behind us. "I love a joke."

I turned to see Tori, a shopping bag in each hand, looking as perfect as ever. She clearly hadn't been for a swim because her hair was all shiny and straight. And her dress was definitely designer. She looked like she was on her way to a fashion shoot, not on a beach vacation.

"Hi," I said, wondering what she was doing here. "What a coincidence, you being at Paradise Point. Small world."

"I'm staying with Persephone," Tori replied flatly. "So, what's the joke?"

My mind raced. *Why was Tori staying with Persephone? Was she a second choice after I let Persephone down?* But that seemed impossible. Surely *I* would be a second choice, not the other way around.

I searched around desperately for a joke I could tell Tori. I certainly wasn't going to explain the whole camping thing to her.

"Er ... I was joking with Mia and Izzy that –"

"What's the joke?" Rio asked, picking up his towel and rubbing himself down. He and Jordan sat down and looked at me expectantly. *Oh great*, I thought, *now I have an entire audience for my camping confession.*

"It's not that funny, actually," I said quickly. "It was more of a private joke."

"Did it have something to do with a food fight?" asked Tori. "Because it looks like you've got jelly in your hair." She leaned in over me. I pulled away, but I could feel everyone's eyes on me. Even Rio was staring at my hair like I had lice. It was the Snow White undies incident all over again!

"We had a jellyfish fight with my brothers on the way here," Izzy explained. "Up there on the headland. They're like ninjas. Fast and merciless."

"Gross!" Tori cried.

The others all laughed, but I was practically dying of embarrassment. I really wanted to impress Rio and Izzy was totally humiliating me. Sometimes she was so clueless.

"Yeah, and that was right after we went looking for a waterfall and got attacked by leeches," Mia laughed. "What a day!"

The guys laughed even harder, but Persephone put her hand over her mouth.

"Leeches?" Tori squealed. "Oh no way. That's, like, totally disgusting!"

I cringed. This wasn't quite how I imagined the afternoon playing out. At least Izzy and Mia hadn't mentioned that we were camping, but I figured it was only a matter of time before they started over-sharing on that subject.

"So, what're you guys doing this week?" I asked, glancing at Rio.

He smiled. He was unbelievably cute.

"Just hanging out. There's not much surf so we might try stand-up paddle boarding. Ever done that?"

"We're going to this amazing restaurant tonight," Tori chimed in, before I had a chance to answer. "It's totally exclusive and always packed with A-listers. My mother's friend owns it. It's going to be so divine."

Izzy rolled her eyes. She obviously wasn't impressed.

"Wow! That sounds really cool," I said.

Tori ignored me. "Probably should be getting back, hey, Percy?" she said. "To start getting ready."

I saw Persephone wince at her nickname. Surely Tori knew she didn't like it.

"But these guys have only just arrived," Persephone said, getting to her feet. "I'm sure we have time for a walk."

As I stood up, I saw Tori staring at my shorts and I remembered they were covered in mud. Not the best look! I hung back, waiting until the guys were up ahead to start walking.

Rio was soon showing off his acrobatics, while Izzy and Mia splashed in the waves. Persephone, Tori and I trailed behind.

Persephone nudged me. "I think Rio's somersault show's for you."

I blushed. "Sure, sure."

"He's always like that," Tori said. "A bit immature for me." She tossed her hair. "Anyway, I want to hear all about the luxury retreat at The Lost World. Percy said you were staying there. Brand-new, is it? What's it like?"

"Um, well, actually it's so unreal that it doesn't exist." I laughed to try to lighten the mood, but no one else was smiling. "We're just staying at the campground. In a tent."

"You don't say," Tori said.

I wasn't sure if Tori was being sarcastic or not, but when I saw Persephone's face fall, I realized she was really disappointed.

I felt like I'd really made a mess of things. I'd ruined any chance of a friendship with Persephone, and I'd let down my friends, too. It looked like I was embarrassed to be camping with them.

"Well, I hope you've got good security," Tori said, half smiling. "Those campers are completely feral, aren't they?"

I shrugged, trying to work out what to say. I could make out that I was a novice camper and didn't belong at The Lost World, which was actually true – that'd keep Tori quiet and improve my friendship chances with

Persephone. Or I could just tell it like it was.

I decided there was only one real option: it was time I told the truth.

"Actually, camping is pretty cool," I said.

Tori groaned. "Nothing good ever happened in a campground."

Persephone didn't say anything, but I could tell she hated the idea of camping, too. It was written all over her face. She wasn't the type of girl to rough it.

Who am I fooling? I thought. *I've got great friends already.* Sometimes they did the most uncool things, but I wasn't that cool myself – especially compared with Tori and Persephone. I was nothing like them.

I saw Rio was way up ahead, wrestling with Jordan. He didn't seem the least bit interested in me, either. I'd probably finished my chances with him as well, by turning up looking like Robinson Crusoe.

Izzy and Mia stopped to inspect something on the water's edge with a stick. It was only when Izzy shouted "Catch!" that I realized what was going on. Izzy hurled a great big blob of jellyfish at me. I stepped aside just in time to see the thing whizz past my ear and hit Persephone smack on the shoulder.

"Eww!" she cried.

I waited for Persephone to totally freak. But instead, she picked up the jelly lump with her bare hands and, with a precise throw, hurled it back, hitting Izzy.

Izzy screamed. I couldn't stop laughing. I never would've thought that perfect Persephone would be such a crack shot with a jellyfish.

"Ewww!" Tori squealed, backing away up the beach.

By this stage Rio and Jordan had discovered the jellyfish supply, too. They pelted each other and then turned on Izzy and Mia, but once Persephone got involved, they were toast.

We ran, squealing and pelting each other with jellyfish and seaweed all the way up the beach. Finally, we declared a truce and ran into the sea, diving under the waves to wash the smelly slime from our hair.

Persephone emerged with a clump of seaweed draped over her head, trying to pass herself off as a mermaid. Then she grabbed the seaweed and hurled it at Jordan. When he dived underwater to grab her legs, she raced out onto the beach.

Tori was standing at the water's edge with her arms crossed when Persephone ran towards her, laughing, and launched another seaweed missile. Tori screamed and backed away, but the seaweed caught her legs.

We all made our way out of the water and Izzy gave Persephone a high five. "Nice shot, girlfriend," she said. "Where did you learn to do that?"

"The advantages of having an older brother are that you get used to disgusting things and you learn to aim straight," said Persephone. By now Tori had marched off up the beach. "Suppose I'd better go and make up with Tori."

"Guess we better get back, too," I said, reluctantly. I'd never realized that a beach fight could be that much fun. But we had to get back. Mia's and Izzy's parents would probably be freaking out by now.

Then Mia came up with an idea. "You guys should all come to our beach tonight. We can build a fire and toast marshmallows."

Rio looked at me for only a moment, but it was long enough to send my mind spinning. Just the idea of sharing a campfire with him was giving me goose bumps. He turned to Jordan, who was already nodding. "Sounds good. Can we bring a couple of friends?"

"Of course," Izzy said.

Persephone looked really disappointed. "Sorry, we have dinner," she said. "I don't think I can make it tonight, but I'll come and find you tomorrow."

I watched with mixed feelings as Persephone and the guys headed off. I couldn't wait to see Rio again, but I was sad that Persephone couldn't hang out with us tonight.

"Persephone's actually pretty cool when you get to know her," Mia said, as we headed back to the campground.

I grinned. Persephone was even cooler than I had imagined.

Izzy nodded. "Yeah, she's great," she said. "But the big question is, which guys will Rio and Jordan bring along tonight?"

As Izzy, Mia and I trudged back to The Lost World, I couldn't stop replaying the moment during our beach war when I'd hit Rio with a sand bomb. He'd stopped and stared at me, looking serious for a second, and then, he'd burst out laughing. So adorable! My body tingled just thinking about it.

Izzy, Mia and I bounced with excitement all the way back to the campground. The rocky headland, with its nasty barnacles and dangerous crevices, seemed like nothing more than a sandbox now that we had a campfire on the beach to look forward to.

I couldn't wait for nightfall.

Chapter Ten

I watched the firelight flicker on Rio's face. I was trying to catch his eye, but his attention wasn't on me.

Rio was watching the seven annoying boys who had taken over our campfire with their sharp sticks and tribal chants.

The Rodent Tribe had turned what could have been the best night ever into a scene from a horror film. At any moment, one of them was going to fall in the fire (if Izzy didn't push one in first), or lose an eye to a flaming marshmallow.

"Mum, tell the boys to get away from the fire," Izzy called. "They won't listen to me."

"Boys, calm down," Izzy's mum halfheartedly called out, and then went back to her conversation.

"But it's *our* fire!" BB shouted in Izzy's face, carrying on with his rodent dance.

It wasn't fair at all. Izzy, Mia and I had put hours of preparation into our campfire event. We had created a seating plan and even a rundown of events:

1. Welcome chat
2. Marshmallow toasting
3. Truth or dare
4. Kissing (optional – depending on the cuteness of the guys who arrived with Rio and Jordan)

We'd been so busy making plans that we'd had to outsource the stick collecting, the constructing and the lighting of the fire to the Rodent Tribe. They'd been happy to help at the time, but now they'd taken over. They claimed the fire was actually theirs. That might have been technically true, but it was totally unjust.

As soon as Rio, Jordan and their two friends had shown up (and been given the big thumbs-up by Mia and Izzy), the Rodent Tribe had descended on us.

They'd completely ignored our seating plan, wedging themselves where they weren't wanted. Then they'd managed to kick sand on everyone by jumping up and down every five seconds.

To make things worse, the parents had parked themselves on one side of the fire. With everything that was going on, it was impossible to get any sort of flow happening with our "welcome chat."

Mia was the only one with any chance at all. She was sitting next to a guy called Tom, who we'd nicknamed TC – short for Too Cute. He and his friend Quade, QC – or Quite Cute – were swimmers who practiced at the same pool as Mia and Izzy, and Mia and TC hit it off right away. I wasn't the only one to notice how well they were getting on.

"Mia's got a boyfriend," one of her brothers called out.

It was just an annoying distraction that Mia chose to ignore until all of the boys joined in. It became a chant, and then the Rodent Tribe incorporated their marshmallow sticks and a few stomps. Soon the whole thing became a full-blown live performance.

"Shut up!" Mia screamed, getting to her feet and running off towards the water.

"You want to look for phosphorescence in the waves?" I asked QC. He'd ended up sitting next to me when the seating plan got screwed up.

He shrugged. "Sure."

"I'll tell Izzy and Mia," I said, "and you tell the guys."

Izzy and I ran to join Mia by the water's edge. She was already inspecting the waves. There was nothing glowing in there, but the sound of the waves crashing on the sand was relaxing after listening to the Rodents and their silly chants. They were still by the fire, singing and waving their sticks in the darkness – too far away to bother us. The guys arrived and I finally found myself standing next to Rio. After all those afternoons watching him on the bus, I could hardly believe that we were standing under the stars together. I couldn't help smiling.

"Have you drawn any dragons lately?" Rio asked. "That one you did with the girl on the bridge was cool."

Being reminded of that terrible bridge-building session made me frown, but it didn't last long.

"I haven't had much time for drawing lately. I've been busy fighting off leeches and jellyfish," I told him, glancing up into his gorgeous eyes. "But I might get a chance to draw another dragon tomorrow. Who knows?"

"So drawing is your thing then?" Rio asked.

"Don't know," I said, shrugging. "I love drawing, but I've never thought about it as 'my thing.' It's just something I do."

"Well, maybe you should," Rio said. "Have you ever thought of being an artist, you know, professionally?"

I scoffed. I wasn't good enough to be an artist, but it was nice of Rio to say so. "You really think I'm okay at drawing?"

"Yeah!" Rio nodded. "You're amazing."

"Really?" I was glad it was dark because I felt my cheeks flush and I was sure I'd gone a lovely shade of red. But inside I was feeling a tiny bit pleased with myself. Everyone told me I was good at drawing. But I'd never believed them, until now. It seemed different coming from Rio. More genuine. Maybe I really did have a future in the art world.

"Thanks," I said, smiling. "That means a lot to me."

We stood in silence for a moment, watching the dark ocean, and I pondered how things had turned out. Only a couple of days ago I'd been too nervous to even talk to Rio, now I was so comfortable with him I didn't feel the need to fill in the silence with chatter. I just enjoyed the moment, letting the waves do the talking for us.

The Rodent Tribe's singing even provided the background music, which seemed kind of cute – until I realized they were singing about us!

Kitty and Rio, sitting in a tree, K-I-S-S-I-N-G. First comes love, then comes marriage …

"Ah …" I scrambled to think of something to say, anything to drag Rio's attention away from the song, but then a voice from behind beat me to it.

"Hey, you guys! What are you doing hiding in the dark?"

Persephone! I ran to give her a hug. "Great! You made it!" I said. "Sorry there are no five-star luxuries over here." I still felt bad for misleading her about the rural retreat.

But she just laughed it off. "Who needs five stars when you've got a million?" She waved her hand at the night sky.

"Where's Tori?" I asked, glancing around.

"She just wanted to hang in the apartment after dinner," Persephone said.

"What? With your parents?"

"With my brother. I think he's the real reason she came to Paradise Point." Persephone looked serious.

"Not much fun for you, then," I said, watching Rio and Jordan kicking a foam float to each other.

"Yeah, bit boring really," Persephone said. "You would have been much more fun."

I felt my insides do a cartwheel. Persephone thought I was more fun that Tori! She didn't think I was a loser for camping or making out we were at a rural retreat. She actually wanted to be hanging out with me.

"Next time," I said.

Persephone grabbed my hand. "Let's not wait for

next time. C'mon. I want to have fun tonight!" She rubbed her hands together like she was preparing for something really exciting. "So, who's up for some Truth or Dare?" she shouted with a wicked smile.

I shook my head in disbelief as everyone gathered around her. We'd been trying to move the party in this direction all night, and Persephone had gotten it sorted out in seconds.

"And it's Lost World rules," Izzy announced. "We're all friends here, so what happens in The Lost World stays in The Lost World."

There was a ripple of excitement as we sat down in a circle to get the game started. I felt so happy. Maybe it was because Rio was sitting so close to me. Maybe it was because I was surrounded by my besties. Whatever it was, I felt like something really special was about to happen. And I was totally ready for it!

"Okay, I'm starting," Persephone said, standing up. "Kitty? Truth or dare?"

I looked at Persephone, my heart nearly jumping out of my chest. I glanced around the circle. Everyone was watching. I didn't look at Rio, but I could feel his eyes on me.

"Truth," I said hesitantly. "No, dare … I mean, truth."

Persephone looked at me with her hands on her hips. "Well, which is it?"

I put my hands over my face, suddenly unable to make a choice. With Rio right beside me, I felt like I was making the biggest decision of my life. Which one should I go for — truth or dare?

If you think Kitty should choose truth, go to page 234.

If you think Kitty should choose dare, go to page 242.

Kitty GOES BACK TO THE CAMP-GROUND *with* Mia *and* Izzy

Chapter Nine

I was relieved to be going back to The Lost World without meeting Rio. I'd never quite been able to believe that Rio was into me. He'd seen me make a complete fool of myself in front of everyone, and then what? He'd been impressed by a dumb drawing? It wasn't that I thought Persephone had lied when she told me all that – it just didn't really make any sense.

Besides, turning up to meet Rio looking like Robinson Crusoe was hardly going to create the right impression. Then there was the whole luxury-retreat story I'd told Persephone. I knew Izzy and Mia wouldn't go along with that for more than about five seconds.

Yes, heading back to The Lost World was saving me a lot of embarrassment. Meeting Rio and Persephone at Paradise Point could have only ended one way: badly.

"Don't worry," said Mia as we scrambled back over the rocks towards The Lost World. "You can see Rio another time."

"Sure," I said. But I wasn't sure at all. I had the feeling I wouldn't see him until school went back.

I had no way to contact Rio or Persephone. I couldn't explain anything until I finally got back to civilization next week and could charge my phone again. But I tried to push that to the back of my mind. Deep down, I knew Persephone was too cool for me anyway. Probably better that I didn't get excited about a friendship that wasn't ever going to work out and a nonexistent boyfriend.

"I say we forget guys and have some fun," I told Mia and Izzy, "just the three of us."

"But what about the cute campers?" Izzy asked.

Mia frowned. "I think they're probably with those girls."

Izzy shrugged, then smiled. "Yeah, whatevs. We don't need guys to have a good time anyway."

"Yeah!" Mia and I both called back.

Linking arms, we balanced on a big boulder and faced the ocean. "All for one, and one for all!" Izzy shouted.

Mia laughed. "Like the Three Musketeers?"

"The Three Musketeers!" Izzy screamed into the wind in a squeaky voice that sounded like Mickey Mouse.

Mia and I joined in with our own silly voices. Izzy did Mickey so well that it sounded like she'd been practicing it for a while.

"The Three Musketeers," we shouted. "All for one and one for all!"

It would have been massively embarrassing if someone had appeared out of nowhere just then, but there was no one around. We had the whole headland to ourselves. We were out of sight of all the perfect people of Paradise Point and all the campers at The Lost World.

We were free from annoying little brothers, free from boyfriend worries and the pressure to be cool. We could be as silly as we wanted.

"Blackmore wears pointy bras!" I shouted at the horizon.

That got everyone laughing.

"Mr. Contra smells like cabbage soup!" Izzy shouted.

"Pickled eggs give me gas!" That was what Mia came up with.

"Then don't eat them!" I shouted back.

"I hate lentil stew!" Izzy screamed.

Before long we were having a random shouting competition. It kept getting crazier, until we were doubled over laughing with tears streaming down our faces.

I couldn't help a thought creeping into my head: *This is the best way ever to get over Rio.* But with that one thought I was thinking of him again. His big brown eyes, his scruffy hair. The way he'd be waiting at the milkshake shop for me to turn up. Was he still there?

As Izzy and Mia stood chatting, I jumped from rock to rock. I poked around and found a soft, yellowish stone in a crevice and used it to draw on a nice flat rock.

Before I knew it, I'd drawn Rio with his scruffy hair, sucking on a straw. Then I drew a girl (a lot like me) sharing the milkshake – her big eyes wide with surprise at how yummy it was. I added a fire-breathing dragon, not for any particular reason, but just because I liked to draw them. Underneath, I wrote the word *LOVE*.

Izzy and Mia both stared at the rock picture when it was finished.

"So cool!" Mia said. "You're so good at drawing. You should be an artist."

I shrugged. "I'm not that good."

"Yeah, you really are," Izzy added. "It's, like, totally your thing."

"Maybe." I'd never thought about it like that before.

"When I think of you, Kitty," Mia said, "I always picture you with a pencil in your hand. You're always drawing something." She looked at my picture on the rocks again. "And you really love drawing dragons, don't you?"

I laughed. "You noticed, did you?"

"Shame the tide will come and wash it off," Izzy

said. "You should have drawn it up there on the rocks at the top of the headland."

"I can always draw another one tomorrow," I told her. Then I turned to the ocean and shouted, "Rio, I think you're the cutest guy that ever rode the 377 bus!"

"You're such a dork, Kit," Izzy said with a chuckle. Then she turned to face the ocean and drew a deep breath. "I love you, cute camper, even though I don't know if your name is Dan or Sam!" Izzy screamed so loudly Dan or Sam probably heard.

Then Mia put her face into the wind. "Tom Cuthbert is a god!"

I was surprised. "Who's Tom Cuthbert?"

"He's a swimmer," Izzy answered. "A really good swimmer. He trains at the pool where we play water polo." She turned to Mia. "Since when have you had a thing for him?"

"I just decided," Mia said, shyly.

"Well, c'mon, Mia," I said, rubbing my hands together. "Tell us everything."

As we walked back to the campground, Mia filled

us in on her romantic interest in the hot swimming star, Tom Cuthbert. He'd had a girlfriend basically forever, but the word on the poolside was that she'd dumped him because he was too serious about swimming. Mia and Tom saw each other at the pool pretty much every afternoon, but Mia didn't really rate her chances with him.

"Just ask him out," I said. "What've you got to lose?"

"Can you even hear yourself?" Mia asked, raising her eyebrows.

I shrugged.

But Mia wasn't going to let me off that easy. "Kitty," she said. "You just ran away from a guy you're totally crazy about because you're wearing dirty shorts. Now you're telling me to ask out a guy I have to work out beside every week. How awkward will it be if he says no?"

"Okay. I get it," I said. "I'm great at giving advice, but not so good taking it."

We finally left the rocks and made our way onto the beach. The cute campers and their girlfriends had a volleyball net set up and were tossing a ball to each other. I wondered if we'd ever be like those girls — having fun hanging out with a group of guys like that. I was kind of jealous, but I smiled as we walked past.

"Wanna play?" one of the girls called out to us. It was the tall one, in a white bikini. She was like an older version of Izzy — all arms and legs that went on forever.

Mia and Izzy were already nodding. They never said no to sports. The tall girl allocated us to teams. Mia and Izzy were on one side. I was on the other. The tall girl then ran through the basics of Lost World volleyball. It was a cross between indoor volleyball and the beach variety, with a few allowances for newbies like Mia, Izzy and me. She interrupted her instructions regularly with "Are you cool with that?" which was actually a pretty cool thing to say in itself. I felt like I was already hooked on the game and we hadn't even started yet.

Then the tall girl introduced everyone. "I'm Hot Dog and this is Red Star, Snoopy, Popeye, Blade ..." She reeled off a bunch of other names that just got wackier as she went along. Izzy, Mia and I just nodded, smiling.

"And what do we call you?" Hot Dog asked.

"That's Mickey Mouse," I said, pointing at Izzy. "And she's Donald Duck." I motioned to Mia. "And I'm Goofy."

Mia and Izzy rolled their eyes at me, looking really embarrassed. I was keeping expectations low with nicknames like that. But the others cheered.

"Way to go!" Popeye (formerly known as Sam, Dan or Calvin) called out. Hot Dog gave me a low five.

"Right back at you, girlfriend," I said, getting into the team vibe.

As we took our places on either side of the net, I eyed Mia and Izzy. I'd been given the job of "spiker babe," which basically meant standing close to the net and blocking the ball if it came near me. There was something else about getting up high and aiming it straight into the ground on the other side, but I was hoping just to get the ball back over the net to start with.

I took a few deep breaths to ready myself. If I'd been doing this at school I would have been nervous, but for some reason I wasn't. I fully expected to be hopeless at volleyball, but it didn't worry me because only Mia and Izzy would know if I played terribly. Well, them and a bunch of hot, but weird volleyball nerds. *Bring it on!* was what I thought.

Hot Dog got the game underway with a colossal serve. She yelled, "Keep it real, people."

The ball bounced around between players on the other side of the net before it came back our way and then went over. I danced from one foot to the other, waiting for the ball to come to me. And then it did.

It was a high shot from Popeye that was about to go straight over my head. I leaped in the air, got my hand over the top of the ball and spiked it. It went down like a bullet on the other side of the net. Red Dog dived to save it, but the ball slammed into the sand, just past his fingertips.

Red Dog rolled over in the sand, stretching his arms out in defeat. "Oh, man!" he moaned as my team erupted in cheers.

My team jumped on me — high-fiving, low-fiving and doing funny handshakes. They were so excited you'd think I'd just won a gold medal at the Olympics.

"Goofy the spiker babe is keepin' it real!" Hot Dog shouted. "Are they legs or steel springs you're bouncing around on?"

Hot Dog collected the ball and returned to the back of the court to serve again. I watched her compose herself and tried to do the same, but my head was exploding with energy. I knew I'd only done one lucky spike, but I felt like I could fly. I'd found a sport I was really good at. Who would have thought it would be beach volleyball!

Chapter Ten

It was almost dark by the time we finally made it back to The Lost World. We were exhausted from our epic volleyball session. As it turned out, my thoughts about a promising career on the national volleyball team had been premature. My star had burned brightly for just a few minutes and then crashed – along with all the balls that I'd spiked straight into the net. Still, I was hooked. I'd definitely be signing up for volleyball when I got back to school. Mia and Izzy agreed that I totally had potential.

When we reached our tent, Mia's and Izzy's families had already started dinner. The boys were sitting at a camp table, their faces covered in ketchup and bits of burned barbequed food. Usually, that sight would have put me off eating altogether, but I was starving. At that moment, a blackened sausage looked gourmet and it tasted even better. After stuffing ourselves, Izzy, Mia and I staggered off to our tent.

I collapsed onto my sleeping bag, moaning, "I can't move. My arms, my legs!"

"My butt," Izzy whined. "How does sand do that?"

That's when I noticed how scratchy my sleeping bag felt. It was full of sand.

"What the –?" Mia began, shaking out her sleeping bag. "There's sand everywhere. How could it get so sandy? We haven't even been in here."

Izzy reached under her pillow and pulled out a gummy snake. "I think I know who's been in here."

"The boys!" we all shouted.

"How come they get candy and we don't?" Mia grumbled.

"How about we fix that, right now?" Izzy grabbed her flashlight and shone it under her face. It made her face creepy, dangerous even. "I think it's time for a raid."

We slipped quietly out of our tent and crept on our hands and knees across the grass. From the amount of noise coming from the big tent, it sounded like the Rodent Tribe were in that one. And by the smell of it, they were having a farting competition. We sneaked past, holding our noses, and slipped into the boys' smaller tent. Izzy shined the flashlight inside. It was a total pigsty, but there was no sign of boys or candy.

"We need a diversion," Mia whispered as we crawled out of the tent.

I knew exactly what to do. "I'll get them out, you two get the loot and we'll meet at the girls' bathroom"

The girls hovered behind the noisy tent while I went into action.

"I'm up for catch and kiss!" I shouted.

Seven boys all screamed at once. They tumbled out of their tent, arms and legs going everywhere. Then they scattered into the darkness squealing "Girls' germs!"

I ran after them. "Oh, come back," I wailed. "I want to kiss you!"

I gave chase for several minutes – long enough for Mia and Izzy to accomplish their mission. Then I tiptoed off to the showers.

Mia and Izzy were waiting there with huge smiles and two big bags full of candy. They waved their loot at me. "We got everything," Mia said.

"And nearly died of suffocation in that stink fog," Izzy said, coughing. She opened her bag and peered inside. "I can't believe how much candy is in here. I wasn't allowed to have *any* candy when I was their age."

"I'm still not allowed," Mia frowned, "because I'm in training." She pulled out a set of pink and white gummy teeth and wore them in her mouth like false teeth. Then she quickly stuffed a gummy pineapple and teddy bear in, too. "These are so good!" she garbled around a mouthful of candy. "Oo on, 'ave some," she said, offering me the bag.

I grabbed a handful and looked around. The showers weren't the nicest place for a late-night candy feast. "Should we go back to the tent to eat these?"

"No way," Izzy said, shaking her head. "That's the first place they'll look for us."

We finally decided the safest place would be the camp kitchen. We scurried across the campground with our stash, like the sneaky little thieves that we were. We fumbled our way into the kitchen, which was in complete darkness, except for the blue glow of a mosquito zapper.

"Don't turn on the light," hissed Izzy. "You'll give us away."

Izzy and Mia found a table and sat at one end. I was just about to sit down when I noticed something.

"Can you see what I see?" I said.

"Doubt it. I can't see a thing," Izzy said, rummaging through her bag. "Including what's in here. I'm not even sure it's candy."

"Over there on the wall," I said. "It's a kettle."

"Oh, hurrah!" Mia said in a posh voice. "Anyone for a nice cup of tea?"

Without explaining, I dashed out of the kitchen. I was super excited about my discovery. A power outlet! Now I could charge my phone! Then I'd be able to text Persephone and, with any luck, see Rio.

I was fumbling with the zip on our tent when a bat flapped overhead. I watched it pass and was suddenly struck by the night sky. The stars were so bright it was like the whole solar system had been amped up.

Then, out of nowhere, a star shot across the sky. A shooting star! *How lucky is that?* I thought. I closed my eyes and wished. I wished for a kiss with Rio. I opened my eyes, hoping Rio would wander out of the darkness and whisper my name. But there was nothing.

I sighed, a little disappointed that the shooting star hadn't worked, and clambered into the tent to find my phone. While I rummaged through my bag, I imagined Rio peering over my shoulder watching me.

"So, what do you think of The Lost World?" I asked him.

Then I did his voice. "Pretty cool. And I especially liked seeing you play volleyball on the beach before. You were smashing it!"

I smiled coyly as I pulled out my charger. "Oh, you are too kind."

The imaginary Rio touched my shoulder. "Really,

you totally rock! You're great at everything. And pretty, too. Babe, you've got it all."

"Oh, Rio. I'm blushing!" I replied.

That was when I caught myself. I put my hand over my mouth to prevent any more installments of the fantasy love scene.

What if Mia's and Izzy's brothers are outside the tent listening? I thought, feeling my cheeks get hot. I would die of embarrassment.

I poked my nose out of the tent to make sure there was no one there. When I was sure I was alone, I flopped back onto my air mattress and stared at my dead mobile. Now that I had a way to charge it, I could get Rio's number and speak to him for real. But was I ready for that?

The imaginary Rio was very easy to talk to, but how would it be if I were actually with him? What would I say? I didn't even know if he liked me. In fact, it was very likely that he didn't, especially after not meeting up with him today.

I was having second thoughts about charging my

phone. If I left it in my bag, Rio would remain in my imagination as the perfect boyfriend. If I charged my phone, something might happen with Rio. It might be good or it might be bad – there was just no way to tell. I felt sure that the shooting star had been a sign: a clue to what I should do. But what had it meant?

Was I supposed to charge my phone or leave it in my bag?

If you think Kitty should charge her phone, go to page 252.

If you think Kitty should leave her phone in her bag, go to page 265.

Kitty TELLS Mia and
Izzy THE TRUTH

Chapter Nine

"What are you doing here?" I said to Izzy to Mia, "I thought you were camping in the middle of nowhere."

Izzy just stared at me. "And I thought you'd hurt your ankle," she said flatly.

Persephone glanced at me sideways and I shuffled uncomfortably. It was bad enough being caught out by Izzy and Mia, but it was total torture facing my friends in front of Persephone. When I told her I'd gotten out of going camping, I hadn't told her that I'd *lied* to get out of it.

"Well," I paused, not exactly sure where to start my explanation. "I don't actually have a sprained ankle."

Mia studied my foot. "But I distinctly remember you telling me you did, and that's why you couldn't come camping."

I took a deep breath. "I'm sorry," I said, and then everything tumbled out of my mouth in a rush. "I really wanted to go on vacation with you two. You're my best friends in the world. But I made up the stuff about my ankle because I didn't want to dig my own toilet or get attacked by leeches or worry about snakes in my sleeping bag. You know I'd be scared senseless on a camping trip like that. And then Persephone asked me to come to Paradise Point, and she said we could meet Rio, and you know I've had a thing for him, like, forever, and I didn't want to upset you guys so I made an excuse not to go camping." I stopped for a breath. "I'm sorry. Really sorry." I looked up at Izzy, Mia and Persephone. "I really am sorry."

Mia put a hand on my arm. "Yeah, we get it," she said. "You're sorry."

I managed half a smile. "So you're not mad?"

Mia shrugged and smiled. "Well, I get why you

didn't want to go camping and –"

"*Of course* we're mad," Izzy interrupted. She glared at Persephone. "And we're mad you decided to go on vacation with …" she paused and, for a terrifying moment, I thought Izzy was going to mangle Persephone's name and call her *stuck-up* right to her face, "… with Per-se-phone. Instead of us."

I breathed a sigh of relief.

"Oh, I feel bad, now," Persephone said. "I didn't know I was stealing Kitty away. Sorry, this must look really terrible."

I could see both Izzy and Mia relax when they heard that. I was stunned, though. It wasn't Persephone's fault that my friends were annoyed with me, but she'd put herself right in the middle of it and apologized. She was definitely a better friend than me.

"You're not to blame," Mia told her and then gave me a smile. "Kitty, we did kind of freak you out with all those camping stories. We might have gone a bit too far."

Izzy said nothing. She just glared at me. I knew she

was still really mad.

"So you're camping at The Lost World?" Persephone asked.

"Yeah, just back over there behind those dunes," Izzy said stiffly.

"So you have to dig your own toilets?" Persephone asked with a frown. "I thought it was nice over there."

"Well, it is," Mia said, finding something on the rocks to look at. "Actually, it's a really beautiful campground. There's a pool and everything."

Now I was totally confused. "What about the leeches and snakes and roughing it?" I asked.

"We made all that up," Izzy said.

I couldn't believe it. *Izzy lied to me? And she wasn't even embarrassed to admit it?*

"Why?" I demanded.

"We wanted you to have low expectations and then surprise you with a nice place. We were thinking of you," Mia said. "We didn't mean to freak you out."

I wasn't sure how I felt about Mia and Izzy's strategy. "Well, it kind of backfired, didn't it?" I said grumpily.

Mia gave me a hug. "We weren't trying to be mean."

"I know," I said. But it kind of felt like they *had* been mean, torturing me with all those camping horror stories. And, yet, now it was me who looked bad because I'd told the lie about spraining my ankle.

At least Mia seemed to have moved on, but Izzy had a face like a cat's bottom. She wasn't the type to forgive and forget. And now Persephone was going to think I was a total loser for lying to my friends.

"I've got an idea," Persephone said. "Why don't we all get together for a sleepover at my place tonight?"

I stared at Persephone. What a cool idea! Doing something fun together would help everyone forget about my stupid lie. And it would give Izzy, Mia and Persephone a chance to get to know each other. I knew Mia would be up for it, but I couldn't tell with Izzy.

"Gee, I don't know," Izzy said, slowly. "I was really looking forward to sleeping on an air mattress that goes down five times during the night."

Mia chuckled. "And then there's the boys," she added. "I really wanted to spend some quality time with my four little brothers. And I really do want to hang out with Izzy's brothers some more, too. They're so cute. Especially BB. I just loved the way he jumped on our tent right after we put it up. So adorable. I just wanted to strangle him."

"Well, if you can tear yourself away from all that," Persephone said with a grin, "come over at seven."

I was feeling slightly stunned. Somehow Persephone had turned the situation around. She must've been some kind of social genius. As I watched her explaining to the girls how to get to her apartment, I knew that she was going to fit into our group without any trouble at all.

We were about to part ways with Izzy and Mia when I remembered that I hadn't even told them the most exciting news of all.

"Guess who we saw on the beach?" I said.

"Rio?" That was Mia's guess.

I shook my head. "Way more famous. An actual celebrity."

"Nemo?" That was Izzy's guess.

I sighed. "That's not a celebrity. It's a cartoon fish."

In seconds Izzy and Mia had turned the whole thing into a guessing game that was already driving me crazy. I took a big dramatic breath to heighten the anticipation. "Kes and Pit!" I shouted.

Izzy and Mia looked at each other. "Who?"

"Kes and Pit," I shrieked, "from The Lads! You really *have* been in the wilderness too long."

"Oh, I thought you were going to say someone really good," Mia said, looking disappointed.

"They are good." I quickly corrected myself. "Well, they were, until we got to know them."

"They're losers," Persephone said, pulling out her phone. She showed Izzy and Mia the photos from our encounter on the beach, including all the pictures of Kes's underarm and the video of Pit's nasal hair.

"Gross!" Izzy sneered.

Persephone laughed. "Yeah, double gross."

I could still hear Mia and Izzy laughing about The Lads as they headed back across the rocks to The Lost World.

Persephone and I hurried back to Paradise Point. It

was almost time to meet Rio and Jordan.

"Izzy and Mia are cool," Persephone said as we scrambled back over rocks. "It's so cute that they tried to give you a nice camping surprise."

"Hmm, suppose so," I said, not totally convinced.

I was relieved, though. That awkward situation with my sprained ankle lie had gone far better than I thought it would. Persephone had been a complete star.

"So you think Izzy and Mia like me?" she asked.

"Yeah, I'd say they do," I said truthfully. My friends really did seem to like her.

I *sooo* couldn't wait until seven that night. It was going to be awesome! So fun to have all of us hanging out together.

Chapter Ten

Persephone sent about ten texts to Jordan on our way to meeting him and Rio. It seemed like she was updating him every few steps with our expected arrival time. If I didn't know her better, I would have thought she was texting because she was nervous. But when she started worrying about what she was wearing, I realized she really was freaking out.

"Should I go back and change into my striped bikini?" she asked. "I'm not really sure about this one. It makes my butt look big."

"You look great, Persephone," I said. "You're just being paranoid."

She frowned. "I don't know. I think I'll just go back and change."

If it had been anyone else going on about their bikini and their butt, I would have been well and truly fed up by now. But coming from Persephone, it was actually a bit of a relief. It made her seem normal. It was like she was even more nervous than me about meeting the guys, if that was possible. Maybe we were just different like that. I was keeping all my worrying inside my head, but hers was pouring out of her mouth.

"Yep," she said, firmly. "We're going back. I have to change."

I grabbed her arm. "If we go back to the apartment, you'll be there for another hour," I told her. "And we're already late to meet the guys."

Persephone hesitated.

"Come on," I said, slipping my arm in hers. "That's the ice cream place where we're meeting them, isn't it?" I pointed just up ahead.

Persephone nodded and managed a half smile.

"All right. So let's go," I told her, grinning.

As we hurried towards the ice cream shop, I realized we were passing the apartment building we'd seen The Lads heading back to earlier. I slowed down to take a look. Sure enough, there was Pit on the balcony, relaxing. I had to admit that he'd look hot if you didn't know he was a total idiot.

That's when I noticed a group of girls gathered on the beach around the apartment building. It certainly looked like The Lads' quiet vacation was already over.

Persephone and I watched as Kes joined Pit on the balcony. We saw he was carrying an armful of colorful balls. He leaned over the balcony.

A moment later I worked out that Kes wasn't holding balls. They were water bombs! Pit and Kes pelted the crowd, sending squealing girls running in every direction.

"Nice guys," Persephone said, sarcastically.

I couldn't help staring. Kes and Pit were both so annoying, but it was Pit who was really bugging me. He was the one I'd swooned over. It was embarrassing to think of that now! I felt totally ridiculous for being so starstruck by such a stupid guy.

I was still staring at Pit when he glanced over and saw me. Then, of all the things, he blew me a kiss!

Gross, I thought. I blew his stupid kiss right back to him in a big, sarcastic way. *What an arrogant loser!*

"Kitty! What are you doing?" Persephone asked, looking shocked.

"I'm being sarcastic," I said.

"That's funny, because, from where I'm standing, it looks like you blew him a kiss."

"Didn't you see how exaggerated it was?" I tried to explain. "That was mocking."

"Possibly a bit subtle for Pit," Persephone replied, "but whatevs. We need to find the guys."

It wasn't hard. They were just behind us, wandering up from the beach. Jordan had a big smile on his face, but Rio looked really awkward.

"So, who's up for ice cream?" Persephone said, clapping her hands.

By the time we got our ice cream, everyone seemed pretty relaxed, even Rio. I was surprised at how comfortable I felt with him, even though I'd been secretly terrified all day. I figured my encounter with those stupid Lads had actually given me a confidence boost.

Jordan and Persephone were so cool with each other that you'd never know how nervous she'd been. She even asked him to try her tiramisu ice cream, and she tasted his butterscotch. It was totally cute. I thought I'd try the same thing with Rio, but he suddenly started to look sick.

"Thanks, but I don't really like chocolate. Or mint."

I thought everyone liked chocolate and mint. I began to wonder if it was me he didn't like.

As we headed to the point, Persephone and Jordan strolled ahead of us. They were nudging shoulders and sharing their ice cream. Rio and I walked stiffly behind them. He'd gone all awkward again. I tried to get him talking about his plans for vacation, but he just gave one-word answers to all my questions. It was the same with school and his family. I did find out his father was a graphic artist, though. That gave us something to talk about because I really liked art, too.

"Yeah, that picture you did in class was really cool," Rio said. "That dragon, I …" He clammed up again. "Let's catch up with the others."

Rio walked off so quickly, I was left wondering what he'd done that he didn't want me to know about, or what I'd done to annoy him. I just couldn't work out why he was acting so strangely.

It wasn't until we got on to the subject of sports that he forgot whatever was bothering him and really came alive. I couldn't believe I hadn't thought of talking about sports before.

Soccer was clearly his passion. He told me he'd be happy to play it all day, every day. Apparently, when he wasn't playing it, he was watching it. He was a massive supporter of Real Madrid, a Spanish team. Then I remembered the sticker on his folder. I kicked myself for not thinking about it earlier. Rio went on about a few other teams in the European competition and then stopped and looked embarrassed.

"Am I boring you?" he asked. "I'm half Argentinean. Soccer's in my blood. *What I can do?*" he said in a really thick accent and then laughed at himself. It was very cute. "So, what kind of stuff do you like?"

I shrugged. I really wanted to tell him I liked sports, but I didn't. I mean, I thought sports were all right, but I wasn't *into* them like Izzy or Mia.

"My friends really love water polo," I told him. "Maybe I'll get into that one day."

"But what about drawing?" Rio asked, with a smile. "I figured that was your thing."

"Oh, yeah," I said, distractedly. "That, too."

I could feel the hair on my neck standing on end as Rio smiled at me. His eyes creased up, just the way I remembered them.

Imagine if he knew I liked drawing HIM, I thought. *He'd probably run for cover!*

For a few glorious minutes, Rio seemed relaxed, which meant I was, too. We stood and watched some kids in the surf, and we talked and laughed about dumb, nothing stuff. At last, Rio seemed to be himself.

Maybe he's been nervous this whole time, I thought, *and now, at last, we're actually connecting.*

Rio even got out his phone to show me a picture of his dog, Pequeño. (He had to spell it out for me.)

"*Pequeño* means 'small' in Spanish," he explained. "But it's a family joke because he's a Rhodesian Ridgeback." Rio showed me a picture of the most enormous dog I'd ever seen.

I told Rio about Sid, my cat. "He brings in dead things from the backyard and leaves them by my bed, so I stand on them in the morning."

I got out my phone, flicking past the dumb photo of Pit and me and loads of school ones until I found my favorite picture of Sid. It was a close-up of his face. He was smoky-gray with a black patch around his eye, a bit like a pirate.

"We should have known when we got him that he'd have attitude," I told Rio, laughing.

I glanced up to see what Rio thought of Sid, but he'd suddenly gotten shy again. He looked at the picture and said, "We should catch up with the others."

I watched him stride off, wondering what had just happened, what I had said to upset him. *Does he really hate cats?* I wondered.

By the time we reached the far end of the beach Persephone and Jordan were practically holding hands while Rio and I had fallen into a silent, single file march.

Something was definitely going on with him. Then it dawned on me. Rio didn't have a thing about cats. He wasn't nervous, or awkward. He didn't have a problem with chocolate ice cream or even mint. *He has a girlfriend.* The more I thought about it the more I knew it had to be true.

Rio was only here to make up the numbers, so Jordan could hang out with Persephone. Rio wanted to be nice to me, because he was a nice guy. But he didn't want to be too nice, because he didn't want to give me the wrong impression. *Maybe his girlfriend has a cat. And that's what made him go all quiet,* I thought.

I sighed forlornly as I realized that the guy I'd been dreaming about for months was completely off-limits. I'd been so excited about spending time with Rio and getting to know everything about him. Now none of that was going to happen. It couldn't – not if he had a girlfriend. I felt crushed, like an elephant had knocked me to the sand and stamped all over my heart. I wanted to run away and hide, and maybe cry a little. But I couldn't. What would Persephone think if I just bolted off without an explanation? All I could think to do was blink back my tears and traipse along after Rio.

I knew I had to find an excuse to get away. I really didn't want to be the one to spoil Persephone's love-in, but I was dying a slow and painful death.

"So, should we get back?" I eventually managed to get out. "Persephone, don't forget you invited Izzy and Mia over tonight," I said, trying to sound upbeat.

Persephone looked at Rio and me. The huge gap between us should have made it pretty obvious what was going on.

"I did, didn't I?" she said, smiling at me and then turning to Jordan. "Well, let's make it a party. Are you guys free tonight?"

Jordan and Rio both answered together, but with opposite replies. Jordan said yes, while Rio's response was no.

He looked so uncomfortable. I felt kind of sorry for him. "Remember, we've got that thing on tonight," Rio said to Jordan.

"But that thing can wait," Jordan said, firmly. He turned to Persephone. "We'll be there. What time?"

Persephone made all the arrangements and outlined the plan for the night: fruit punch cocktails by the pool, then pizzas and a DVD. I would have loved that plan at any other time, but right at that moment it sounded worse than a three-hour algebra test.

"See you tonight," Persephone called out as the guys headed off the other way down the beach.

Jordan grinned at her and waved at me. Rio could barely manage a nod.

"What's up with Rio?" Persephone asked as we headed back to her apartment. "Did he swallow a bee or something? I used to think he was really nice, but he was being an idiot just now."

"Luckily, Jordan made up for it," I said, trying to hide my disappointment. "You two look really cute together."

Persephone smiled, but then looked at me seriously. "Sorry things were awkward with Rio. I don't know what happened."

"Did Jordan say anything?"

"Nothing about you and Rio," she said, shaking her head. "Strange, hey? Unless … do you think there's another girl involved?"

I nodded. "That's exactly what I think. He was actually starting to chill until I showed him a picture of my cat."

Persephone frowned. "Huh?"

"His girlfriend probably has a cat," I explained. "Anyway, so I guess it's all over for me."

"What? Really? You're just giving up?"

"Well, I'm not chasing after a guy who's not into me," I told Persephone.

"No, of course not. You don't have to chase him," she said. "But maybe there's something else you could try."

Chapter Eleven

"You know how I said to be yourself and Rio will like you?" Persephone said, holding a pair of sparkly silver shorts up against me. "Well, forget all that. Let's try something different."

"Hot pants aren't going to change how Rio feels about me," I said flatly.

Persephone threw the shorts on my bed and went through her closet, looking for a top to go with them. "No, but I bet they'll work on my brother."

"Aren't I trying to impress Rio?" I asked, feeling confused.

Persephone shook her head. "The new plan is to

make Rio jealous. So you're going to ignore him all night and talk to my brother instead. Then, Rio will realize what a catch you are and swoop in!"

"Have you tried this tactic before?" I asked, doubtfully.

"Sure. Tori does it all the time," Persephone said.

"And how does it go?"

Persephone thought for a moment. "Well, mixed results." She must have seen my frown, because suddenly she sounded way too enthusiastic. "More good than bad, actually. And I think we've got a great shot tonight, because we're in control. It'll be like starring in our own movie. We've got the venue, chosen the actors, designed the costumes, and we know how it's all going to end. You and Rio together, just how it should be!"

"And if it doesn't work out like that?" I said, holding up the hot pants.

Persephone brushed the idea away as she threw a cute little top at me and then began to run a straightener over her hair. "It has to. Look, I don't find acting that easy either. But if that's what it takes for you and Rio to be together, it has to be done."

I could totally understand why Persephone was so keen to make things work between Rio and me. It wouldn't be fun for anyone if we were moping around while she and Jordan were trying to have fun. I had reservations, though. I didn't want to come between Rio and his girlfriend.

But Persephone didn't believe it could be anything serious. "If Rio had a serious girlfriend, I'd know about it," Persephone said. "Jordan would have said something. Even Rio would have said something. No, if Rio has a girlfriend, this is very new."

Persephone was convinced something had happened during the afternoon to change Rio's mind about me. So we went back through Jordan's texts. It seemed clear Rio had been keen to hang out when the texts came through, but then, a couple of hours later, something had changed. We figured he must have bumped into someone he knew on the beach – or met someone he wanted to get to know.

"It just can't be serious at this stage," Persephone

said as she chose a nail polish to go with her orange top. "And we made our date with the guys first, so basically, Kitty, some other girl is muscling in on your guy."

I looked in the mirror, applying lip gloss. "I guess so."

Rio's girlfriend wasn't my only concern about our plan. Our biggest problem was making it actually work. To make Rio jealous, George had to be interested in me. I didn't think there was much hope of that, whether I was wearing silver hot pants or not.

"You've got to think like an actress," Persephone coached. "Play the part. Don't just talk the talk, you've got to walk the walk."

"What does that mean?" I asked, totally confused.

Persephone shrugged. "Actually, I have no idea," she said. "It's what Dad says when he wants me to put more effort into something."

Persephone paused to run her fingers through her perfect, glossy hair. "Look, I'm acting already – I'm being my father." She stood on her toes and stuck out her tummy and frowned. "Now, go to bed and don't have any fun, ever," she said in a deep voice. "And you're grounded for the rest of your life. With no allowance!"

I gave her a clap. "Bravo!"

Persephone took a bow. "Now, it's your turn to act."

"Who should I be?"

Persephone thought for a bit. "Try Tori. She normally gets her own way."

I thought for a bit. I had no idea how to act like Tori. If I had a choice, I'd play Persephone. She was cool and fun, and guys loved her. But I couldn't say that — it would sound too weird. "Guess I'm Tori then," I said.

As we finished getting ready, we went through the plan one more time. Persephone and I agreed that nothing could be left to chance. The whole night had to be scripted from the moment everyone arrived until the second the guys left. We had to know when to stand, when to sit, when to talk and when to listen. The whole night had to work.

Persephone had even briefed her mother to let the guys and Izzy and Mia into the apartment and show them outside to the pool area, where we would be waiting with fruit punch cocktails.

The pool area was shared by all of the apartments in the building, but Persephone and her family were the only ones who ever used it. It was like an exclusive private party venue, overlooking the beach.

"This is going to be the best night ever," Persephone said, dragging the last of the lounge chairs into place and spreading frangipani flowers around them. She lit the candles and then lined up the punch glasses and decorated them with tiny umbrellas.

I would have helped her, but I was busy practicing walking in Persephone's wedges. They looked amazing, but they were hard to master.

"No one said this was going to easy," Persephone called as I wobbled across the terrace for a third time.

In the end, Persephone gave the idea the thumbs-down. She was sure I would fall into the pool, ruin my chances with Rio and ruin her wedges in the process.

Once everything was ready, we practiced reclining like movie stars on the lounge chairs. It was harder than it looked. Persephone leaned so far back that she tipped the chair over. Then I did something wrong and the whole thing collapsed under me. I was still trying to get untangled when we heard the buzzer at the apartment.

"No one's meant to be here for another three minutes!" Persephone gasped, with a panicked look on her face. Quickly, she smoothed her hair and ran for her lounge chair. "I'm in this one, and you're over there next to the cocktails."

I frowned. "Wasn't I going to be next to you when the guys arrived and then move to the one next to the cocktails, so Jordan could be next to you?"

Persephone's eyes darted from one lounge chair to the other. "That's right! Quick, into place!"

She stretched out and I raced to the lounge chair beside her. I got there just in time to see Persephone's brother, George, come through the pool gate with a couple of guys, all in board shorts.

That so *wasn't* part of the plan! George had been told to wait until Rio and Jordan had arrived to come to the pool, and he wasn't meant to bring friends!

I glanced over at Persephone. She was no longer

reclining like a movie star. She was sitting up, glaring at George, looking very much like an angry sister.

"Hey, what are you guys doing here?" she demanded. "You're not supposed to be here now."

"Whadda ya think, Percy Pony?" George said calmly, tossing his towel on the lounge chair that had been allocated to Rio. "We're going for a swim."

Persephone jumped to her feet, swept George's towel off the chair and threw it on the one George was meant to be using. "But I told you −"

George didn't wait to hear any more. He did a massive dive-bomb and his friends followed. Seconds later the terrace was awash with drowning frangipani flowers and dead candles. I was soaked and Persephone was furious.

"You're *so* grounded!" she yelled at her brother. Somehow Persephone had dropped the movie star role and picked up the dad role. But the guys didn't notice. They were too busy yelling and wrestling each other in the pool.

It was too noisy to hear anything, which is why we

didn't notice Rio and Jordan arriving until they opened the pool gate.

Persephone sighed as she watched them come in, a trickle of mascara running down her face. "What timing," she muttered.

Our perfectly scripted romance was turning into a disaster movie.

Chapter Twelve

Persephone was still looking dazed as Jordan and Rio strolled across the terrace towards us. I couldn't blame her. Everything we'd worked on all afternoon had been for nothing. The pool was trashed. We were both standing instead of lounging, my hair was a mess and Persephone looked less than perfect.

The rest of the plan wasn't working either. George hadn't noticed me or my hot pants, and even though I was supposed to be ignoring Rio, I couldn't take my eyes off him. He looked even cuter than before in his purple T-shirt. As he came closer, I couldn't help hoping that it wasn't a girlfriend that had been getting in our way. Maybe Rio did just really hate cats.

"Made it," Jordan said. He gave Persephone a kiss on the cheek. "Thanks for inviting us."

Persephone's face lit up. "Oh, just a little poolside gathering. We haven't gone to any trouble."

Rio smiled at Persephone and then turned to me. "Nice party."

"We've made fruit punch cocktails!" I said far too brightly. I handed everyone a drink, even though Persephone was supposed to be playing hostess. "Here's to great vacations!" *What was I saying?*

I was just taking a sip when a ball sailed towards us. Rio stretched out his arm and caught it with one hand, then hurled it back into the pool. *Just like on the bus*, I thought, forlornly.

"Hey, Rio!" yelled one of the guys in the pool. "Come in. You too, Jordan."

Persephone frowned. "You know my brother and his friends?"

Rio nodded. "They're in my brother's year at school."

Persephone groaned. "You should definitely have a game with them, then."

Rio didn't need any encouragement. He stripped off his top. He was tanned and muscly, but not super muscly. Yep, Rio was definitely good-looking. I felt my cheeks get hot as he dive-bombed in.

"I was actually being sarcastic," Persephone muttered, as she watched Jordan bomb in after Rio.

"That could have gone better," I said, as we sat together on our wet lounge chairs. I gulped down my drink in one mouthful. There just didn't seem much point sipping it elegantly while keeping my toes pointed, like I'd practiced.

Persephone was watching the pool. "Don't worry. We can get things back on track. We just need George to get out of the pool and sit next to you, Rio to move over there and Jordan ..." She glanced between the chairs. "Where were Izzy and Mia going to sit again?"

"I'm not sure it really matters. Rio just isn't into me," I said sadly. "He hardly even looks at me. He's definitely got a serious girlfriend. Just forget about it.

You go have fun with Jordan. I'll be okay."

"No way!" Persephone said. "We've still got a good chance to get things going when we sit down to watch the movie. You'll see."

I smiled at Persephone. She really was trying to help, but I knew Rio was a lost cause.

Tonight, I'll just hang out with Izzy and Mia, I decided. They had just arrived and were waving at us from the apartment balcony.

"Come down!" Persephone called.

The girls soon appeared and raced across the terrace to give us a hug. "This is so cool," Mia said, beaming.

I handed them each a punch.

"Wow! Things are so sophisticated over here at Paradise Point!" Izzy put on a posh voice and held her little finger out as she sipped her drink. "La dee da!"

I shot a glance over to Persephone, and was glad to see she laughed it off.

"Would you like to try our canapés? We made them specially. Chips *à la mer*." Persephone grinned as she passed around a bowl of sea salt chips.

"Don't mind if I do!" Izzy said in her posh voice.

Just as Izzy reached for the chips, one of the guys jumped in the pool, spraying us with water. Izzy looked down at her hand, which was now in a bowl of cold chip soup. She glared at the pool. The guys had set up some shoes as goals at each end of the pool and were having a game of water polo.

"This means war," Izzy said, flicking the sticky, wet chips from her fingers.

She stripped down to her bikini and waited for us to do the same.

Mia followed quickly. "Coming in?" she asked me.

"We actually need your help here," I said.

Mia looked around. "You want me to get some more chips from upstairs?"

"No," I whispered. The girls edged closer, so we were in a four-way huddle. "We need some help to get Rio to fall madly in love with me. We've got a plan and we need you to be part of it. You just need to do a bit of acting."

Izzy snorted. "Sounds fun. Not! But, don't worry, I'll

be in the pool if you need me."

I watched her race off and jump into the pool.

"I think she's still mad that you lied about spraining your ankle," Mia explained. "But I'll help. I can be an actor in the pool."

My heart sank as I watched Mia jump into the pool, too. What a pair of fish they were. If they saw a pool, they had to be in it.

I turned to Persephone. She stood staring glumly at her cocktail. Somehow a frangipani had managed to find its way into her drink. It floated around with a soggy, mini umbrella.

"What happened to our script?" she moaned softly.

I took the cocktail gently from her hand and flicked the flower and umbrella pieces out of her drink. "What are we doing wrong?" I asked.

She shrugged. "Everything."

I sat back on my lounge chair to assess the situation. Everyone in the pool was getting on just fine. At least that was a good start. Rio laughed as he tossed the ball past Izzy to one of George's friends, Levi. He was a big athletic-looking guy, definitely Izzy's type. Interesting. Mia was jumping on top of one of the other guys. Not scripted, but a nice touch.

Then my eyes went back to Rio and, even though I tried, I couldn't look away.

I knew I was still hopelessly smitten. And I didn't *want* to get over him. I really wanted to be laughing with him, sharing a joke, talking about important things, talking about stupid, nothing things.

Persephone's plan was my only hope of that ever happening. And if Rio was still in a good mood when he got out of the pool, maybe we had a shot at making it work.

Beside me, Persephone sighed. "Let's just forget the script and join everyone in the pool. It looks like more fun than we're having."

But I just wasn't sure that I wanted to give up yet. "Maybe we should give the plan a bit longer. We haven't really given it a chance to work yet."

Persephone shrugged. "Up to you, but we're missing out on a game of water polo."

I stared at Rio, trying to work out what was the best course of action. Should I trust the plan to win over Rio, or should I just abandon the script and have some fun in the pool?

If you think Kitty should stick to the plan, go to page 273.

If you think Kitty should abandon the plan, go to page 289.

Kitty KEEPS LYING about HER ANKLE

Chapter Nine

"Well, this is a surprise," I said, lifting my right foot off the ground to add credibility to my sprained-ankle story. "I thought you two were camping in the middle of nowhere."

"We are," Izzy said, studying my ankle. "Over at The Lost World. There's a campsite there."

"I've heard it's really beautiful," Persephone said.

"Yeah, if you like digging your own toilets and don't mind leeches and snakes," I said with a laugh.

Persephone glanced sideways at me, giving me a *what on earth's going on* look. I had my hand resting on her shoulder to give the impression that she was supporting me. I hoped she'd work out what was happening before she blew my cover.

"It's not that bad, is it?" Persephone asked Izzy. "I heard that The Lost World is really nice and has a pool. I didn't know you had to dig your own toilets."

Izzy and Mia looked at each other for several moments and then turned to us. "You don't," said Izzy.

"What do you mean?" I demanded, standing up straight before I remembered I was supposed to be injured. I slumped back on Persephone, almost knocking her off the rock we were sharing.

"Looks like you're really suffering with that ankle," Mia said.

I nodded. "It's not too bad, but I think I was a bit ambitious trying to climb around this headland."

Izzy rolled her eyes. "It's insane," she said. "You should get it checked out and strapped up. You've probably made it worse trying to walk on it. It looks really puffy." Izzy bent down to inspect my ankle. "Mind you, the other one does, too. Probably because your ankles are a bit on the chunky side."

"Hey!" I said. But I didn't protest too much. Izzy was buying the sprained-ankle story, so I didn't want to push it.

"I feel bad now," Mia said, looking forlornly at my foot. "We actually thought you were lying about your ankle when we saw you sitting on the rocks. I mean who comes out here with a sprained ankle?"

"Yeah," I said. "How dumb am I?"

"Really dumb," Persephone said.

I frowned, but I couldn't say anything. I knew I'd put Persephone in a really awkward position, expecting her to go along with my lie. I had to be grateful she was doing that, and just put up with any insults that came with it.

Persephone waved her finger at me. "I said it was a crazy idea. But you just wouldn't listen."

"I feel bad about something else, too," Mia said, chewing her bottom lip. "We made up all those terrible camping stories. The Lost World *is* a really nice campground."

"Why would you do that?" I said, hobbling after Persephone who seemed to be edging away from me.

"We wanted to give you a nice surprise when you got there and saw how great it was," Mia explained. "You'd really like it over there."

"Really?"

Mia nodded.

I looked away, starting to feel guilty. I'd lied to my best friends to get out of a horror camping trip with them. But as it turned out, they had actually planned a nice surprise for me. I really couldn't tell them the truth, because it would look like I changed my mind because I had a better offer. And I wasn't going to improve things by sticking around chatting with Izzy and Mia. It was awkward, pretending to hobble and worrying what Persephone was going to say next. I just wanted to get away.

"Shame about your ankle," Izzy said. "The Lost World is really cool. Anyway, looks like you're going to have fun at the beach with … Per-se-phone."

I gritted my teeth. Sometimes my friends could be so uncool. Izzy had nearly mangled Persephone's name right in front of her. I needed to escape before things got worse. Izzy might decide to tell Persephone she was stuck-up or something.

"Yeah, such a shame I couldn't go camping," I said, trying to wrap things up. "But I'd be no fun with a sprained ankle anyway. I just wouldn't be able to keep up with you two."

Persephone glared at me, but thankfully didn't say anything.

"So, anyway, nice to see you," I said. "Better get going. We're meeting Rio and Jordan for an ice cream on the beach. And it's going to take me forever to get back."

Mia crossed her fingers. "Good luck with that, Kitty. Sounds really cool."

"Yeah, we better go, too," Izzy said. "We've got some boys to get back to as well. Sadly, they're all under twelve and totally feral."

"And we're related to them." Mia added.

"How many brothers do you have?" Persephone asked.

"Seven between us," Izzy said.

Persephone laughed and gave Izzy and Mia a fist

bump. "Respect, girlfriends. I've only got one brother and he drives me crazy."

I frowned at the impromptu bonding session. I should have been happy to see Izzy, Mia and Persephone laughing together. Instead I felt flat and suddenly wished I had a brother to complain about, too.

"So, see you around," I said, hobbling off.

Mia shrugged. "Well, I don't have a phone with me and Izzy's is dead, so I guess we'll just see you back at school."

"Hey!" Persephone said excitedly. "Why don't we meet you tomorrow at Paradise Point?"

Inside I was groaning. I loved to hang out with Mia and Izzy, but this was getting more awkward by the second. If we met them tomorrow I'd have to keep up the limping act. They were going to work it out eventually, and I'd look really bad.

Before I could think of a reason why we couldn't meet up with them, Persephone had it all worked out. She gave Izzy and Mia the details of where and when to meet and waved them off.

"I like your friends," Persephone said as I hobbled alongside her on our way back to the Paradise Point.

I glanced over my shoulder to see if Izzy and Mia could still see me. When they disappeared from view, I dropped my hand from Persephone's shoulder and sighed. It was a relief to be able to walk without a limp again. "Glad that's over."

"That was really scary," Persephone said.

"Yeah," I agreed. "I was worried they'd work out what was going on."

"No, Kitty." Persephone stopped and stared at me. "I meant you. You're such a good liar it's scary. You could teach a class on lying and even Tori would have to take notes."

I flinched at her words. Being told that I was a better liar than Tori was harsh. I had tried to do the right thing by lying about my ankle to protect my friends' feelings. But Persephone had a point and now I was really feeling guilty.

"I should have told the truth, huh?" I asked Persephone.

She shrugged. "What do you think?"

I sighed. I'd really screwed things up now – not only with Izzy and Mia, but also with Persephone. She was too nice to get mad at me, but I could see she was looking at me differently.

"I feel so, so bad," I said, looking out to sea. "I just panicked. I should have told them the truth. But, I don't know, the wrong thing came out." I turned to Persephone. "Sorry I put you through that. Thanks for being, you know …"

"A good liar?"

"Yes. I mean, no. Not a good liar …" I tried to think of the right words. "I mean someone who can keep a secret. Oh, it's all coming out wrong." I put my hands over my face, taking a moment to get my thoughts in order. Then I looked at Persephone again. "Thank you for being a good friend. Sorry I lied, and sorry you had to lie, too. You've got to believe me. I feel terrible about that."

Persephone was smiling. "I take it back," she said. "You're not like Tori at all. Look how confused and remorseful you are! Tori would have me believing

I started the lie. Then I'd be the one apologizing and feeling bad."

I smiled, relieved that Persephone had forgiven me. And I was really glad to hear that I was nothing like Tori, after all.

"When we see Izzy and Mia tomorrow, I'll tell them everything," I promised her as we continued our walk across the rocks.

Persephone nodded. "Yeah, we should do something nice to make it up to them. We could go to the new sushi train."

"I still can't believe they told me I was going to have to dig my own toilet, just to surprise me," I said, shaking my head.

"They were really sweet doing that for you," Persephone said. "I don't know anyone who'd do that for me. I never get surprises."

"Not even from your brother?"

Persephone frowned. "What?"

"He never comes around the corner and screams SURPRISE?"

My yell must have *really* surprised her because she lost her balance, slipped and fell onto me. Unfortunately, it happened just as I was trying to negotiate a tricky section on the rocks. I stumbled backwards and fell off a boulder. I howled. It felt like a shark had bitten off my leg! I looked down and realized my ankle was trapped in a crevice. Persephone helped me wriggle it free, but then the pain got worse.

"Oh, no!" Persephone said, peering at my foot. "It looks like you've sprained your ankle."

"I feel so bad," Persephone said when we finally made it off the rocks and back to the beach. It was about the fiftieth time she'd said it.

"It's not your fault," I said, also for the fiftieth time. "I shouldn't have surprised you."

"I think you should go to the hospital," Persephone said.

I shook my head. "Come on, the guys are waiting

for us." I wasn't being a martyr, I just didn't think it was that bad. I knew it wasn't broken.

"You sure?" Persephone said, looking worried.

"Well," I said, smiling. "I could do with a bit of help."

Persephone waited while I put my arm around her neck. I instantly felt relief at getting some weight off my ankle. Maybe I really had sprained it. I'd have to find a doctor tomorrow if it hadn't settled down by then.

In the meantime, I hobbled along, dreaming of Rio to keep my mind off the pain. I was trying to visualize him in the ice cream shop, his hair all scruffy from surfing. He'd smile when he saw me and ask which flavor I liked.

I turned to Persephone. "Do you think it sounds corny to ask for a 'single scoop of Rio'?"

She laughed. "Kitty, I think the pain's getting to you," she said. "*Do not* ask for a single scoop of Rio. Just be yourself. Don't try too hard."

I nodded, exploring some other options in my mind. I needed to come up with an opening line for Rio – one that looked like I wasn't trying too hard, but was actually going to knock him over. The name Rio seemed like a pretty obvious place to start. It meant "river" in Spanish and Portuguese. It was the capital of Brazil — Rio de Janeiro, which meant the River of January. (Yes, I had done my research.) I was just about to run another idea by Persephone, when, out of nowhere, Rio and Jordan appeared.

"What happened to your leg?" Rio asked, pushing his hair away from his face.

I was all ready to explain about my sprained ankle when something happened. As I gazed into Rio's concerned eyes, I forgot my injury and my worries about opening lines. Even the nerves that I'd been carrying from watching him on the bus for the past few months all drifted away with the sea breeze. It felt like Rio and I were the only people on the earth.

I opened my mouth but no words would come out. There was a sickening knot in my stomach. I dropped my eyes to the sand and froze.

We stood there not talking, until Persephone saved me from myself.

"Kitty's in a lot of pain!" Persephone said. "She caught her ankle in the rocks."

I glanced up at Rio. He was looking at me, with a slight smile on his face.

I dropped my eyes to the safety of the sand again and shuffled uncomfortably, still clinging to Persephone's shoulder.

"Maybe you should get that checked out," Rio said, bending down to inspect my ankle.

"It's nothing," I mumbled, staring down at his messy hair. I just wanted to get away. I didn't need him poking around at my purple foot. "Really, I'm fine." I unwrapped my arm from Persephone's neck and took a step sideways to prove my point. "See."

Instantly, I toppled and landed in the sand, face first.

"Ew!" I groaned, spitting out gritty sand, but I was in no hurry to move. I just lay there with my eyes closed. Maybe if I stayed really still, the others might leave me to my humiliation and go for an ice cream without me. I waited, hopefully, for a few moments. Then I heard Rio say, "Do you need some help?"

I rolled onto my side, wiping sand from my face. Rio was kneeling beside me, but I ignored his offer of help, and shuffled onto my bum. I just felt too embarrassed to even look at him.

"All good, thanks," I said, managing a tiny smile.

Persephone rolled her eyes. "Kitty, I think you're the most accident-prone person I've ever met," she said with a smile. "But, hey, it could have been worse. A seagull might have flown over and pooped on your –"

"Please," I put my hand up to stop her finishing the sentence, "don't even say it."

I got up on my elbows to look at the sky and make sure it wasn't actually going to happen. Seagulls were flapping all over the place, but thankfully none were flying over my head.

I wondered how I had turned a perfectly normal injury into the second-most embarrassing moment of my life. Or was it the most embarrassing? Either way, Rio must have thought I was a total idiot.

"So, who's up for ice cream?" Persephone asked, getting to her feet. She was obviously trying to get things back on track. The guys both nodded. But I'd suddenly lost my appetite.

I wasn't sure if it was the fall or the humiliation that came with it, but my ankle was throbbing.

"I think I might need to see a doctor after all," I told Persephone. "But you go ahead. I'll call you when I'm done."

Persephone looked at me, worried. "Don't be silly. I'll take you. We can see the guys tomorrow."

I saw Jordan's face fall. He was probably hoping for a very different afternoon to the one that was playing out. "Yeah, tomorrow —"

"I can take Kitty," Rio interrupted. He stood up and stretched out his hands to me. "There's a medical clinic right across the road."

I stared at his hands for a few seconds, before I felt brave enough to look at his face. "No, it's fine. Thanks, Rio," I said. "I can go on my own."

But Rio didn't seem to hear. He grabbed my hands and pulled me to my feet. Then, before I had time to work out what was happening, Rio had my arm around his neck and I was hobbling awkwardly towards the doctor's office.

I glanced back over my shoulder. Persephone and Jordan were smiling and waving from the ice cream shop.

Chapter Ten

Rio released me into a chair in the busy medical center. He handed me a magazine, gave my details to the receptionist and then sat down next to me.

"All right?" he said, smiling.

"Much better," I said, trying to work out what was going on behind his smile. Surely he thought I was a major loser, and was annoyed about having to spend the afternoon waiting to see a doctor. I searched his face for signs of irritation, but he looked quite content as he reached for a fishing magazine and started flicking through the pages.

"Thanks," I whispered. "You're really sweet."

Rio looked up from his mag. Our eyes met for no more than a second or two, but it was long enough. I felt myself falling, my heart racing, my mind spinning. Who would have thought that a sprained ankle could be romantic?

I glanced away to compose myself, watching a boy who had just walked in. He had blood on his face from a gash on his forehead. My euphoria vanished. "What a way to spend a vacation."

"Yeah. Hopefully you're fine," Rio replied, "and it's nothing too serious."

I nodded. "Hopefully."

Rio glanced back at his magazine for a second, and then closed it. "I was out for most of the soccer season with a broken foot last year," he said.

I winced. "Sounds painful."

"It was. And really, really annoying." He hesitated. "Even though it was actually my own fault."

"Why? What happened?"

Rio looked away for a second and then told me the whole story. It was the first game of the season and he'd "taken a dive," which apparently meant making a tackle look worse than it was by falling to the ground. He'd been trying to force a penalty in front of the goal mouth. He ended up getting the penalty, but by diving he'd also managed to break his foot. "I guess I got what I deserved."

I was surprised; it was almost exactly what had happened to me. I glanced at Rio, wondering if I should share my story, too. But I pushed the idea away. He'd just get the wrong idea about me. It was one thing to fake an injury on a soccer pitch to help your team out. It was another to lie to your friends. So, instead, I focused on soccer.

"Big fan of Real Madrid, are you?" I asked, making use of the bit of intel I'd picked up from his folder in the bridge-building session.

Rio raised his eyebrows. "Is it that obvious?"

I smiled coyly. "The sticker on your folder at school gave you away."

Rio laughed and then talked more about soccer, his friends and his brother, who were all as crazy about soccer as he was. Rio lived and breathed soccer from the sound of it. Not that he really had a choice, he said. Because his dad was Argentinean, soccer was basically in his blood. That explained Rio's slight and very cute accent.

"Shame I didn't inherit my dad's artistic skills, though," Rio said, sighing. "He's a graphic artist. He's got an amazing imagination."

"What sort of work does he do?"

"Really modern stuff. Totally offbeat. A bit like him really. It's hard to describe. I'll have to show you sometime."

I felt my heart skip a beat as he said the words. Rio was inviting me to see his dad's work. I could barely believe what I was hearing.

I couldn't help a smile spreading across my face. "That'd be cool."

Rio glanced at his hands. "You're going to think I'm a complete stalker," he said slowly, "but remember that bridge picture you drew with the dragon?"

I laughed. "How could I forget!"

"Well, I rescued that picture out of the trash and took it home to show it to my dad. He thought it was really good. You're really good."

I felt myself blush. "It was nothing. Just a doodle," I said. "I'm not that good. Anyway, you're not a stalker. I'm the one …" I took a deep breath to stop myself from saying any more. I was just about to blurt out my own stalker story. I knew Rio would run for the exit if he knew I'd been studying him on the bus practically every day. I scrambled for something sensible to say. "I haven't told you the whole story about my ankle," I said before I'd had a chance to work out if now was the right time for a confession. And then it all just came out. Every last terrible detail. "Probably got what I deserved, huh?"

I waited for Rio to judge me, feeling totally exposed. I'd probably made a terrible mistake telling him that I'd lied to my friends. He'd think I was completely two-faced. But he just shrugged.

"Don't beat yourself up. We've all done it. You were just trying to protect your friends' feelings."

"Yeah, I was," I said. "But I guess I got what I deserved."

I looked down at my ankle. It was still throbbing, and looked worse than ever. Somehow, though, it didn't really feel like a punishment anymore. I felt like I'd won first prize in some cute-guy lottery. I was sitting inches away from Rio, the guy I'd been dreaming about for months. I knew everything about his face, his hair, the way he moved, and the way he laughed from watching him on the bus. But now I was actually getting to know him.

I glanced at Rio's face. He caught me watching, but instead of looking away, he just smiled.

"What?" he asked, even though he must have known exactly what I was thinking.

"Kitty MacLean," someone called.

I looked up, startled. I'd almost forgotten where I was until I stood to walk. *Oh, the pain!*

Rio helped me into the doctor's exam room. She checked me over, squeezing and prodding my foot and ankle. She didn't think it was broken but she told me to have an X-ray if it didn't get better in a couple of days. She sent me on my way with a bandaged ankle, crutches, instructions on painkillers and a stern telling off for playing around on the rocks.

I felt like a naughty three-year-old. I glanced at Rio, who was trying to hide a smirk. I elbowed him, but it only made him snort, which gave me the giggles. The doctor frowned as I thanked her and shuffled out of the exam room, trying unsuccessfully to keep a straight face.

I was still smiling right up until the moment that the receptionist cleared her throat, and I realized that I had to pay a bill.

"Seventy-five dollars for today's visit, thank you."

This was exactly what my mum had in mind when she gave me an "emergencies only" stash of cash. Just a shame I had spent most of it on bikinis. My heart was in my mouth as I pulled out the last of the money from my wallet. Thirty-five dollars. I unzipped the change section and counted out my coins.

The receptionist stared at me and tapped her pen. "Is there a problem?"

I scrambled through my wallet one more time. And

then I saw a bulge in a side pocket that I never used. I opened it up and pulled out a roll of twenties and a note. It read "ABSOLUTE Emergencies Only." *Thank you, Mum!*

"No problem," I said, smiling at the receptionist and handing her the cash.

Rio gave me a cheeky smile as he opened the door to the medical center so I could hobble out on my new crutches. "Thought we were going to have to wash the floors to get out of there. What a first date!"

I almost fell off my crutches. *First date? Rio thinks this is a first date?*

I looked up at him, smiling, trying to play it cool. "Oh, I really know how to have fun. I never stop."

"So," Rio said, as we stood on the footpath still looking at each other. "We should find the others."

"Yeah, totally." I nodded, but neither of us moved. It was like we were held in a date spell. If we moved, the magic would all be over. I studied Rio's face, unable to do anything, until I heard someone calling me.

"Kitty, is your ankle okay?"

I managed to drag my eyes away from Rio and saw Persephone and Jordan running across the street. They looked so cute, hand in hand.

"I'm totally okay," I said, feeling dazed. "Amazing. Couldn't be better."

It was true, but I wasn't talking about my ankle. I'd never felt so good inside.

Chapter Eleven

"What's it like to be in love?" I asked Persephone as we lay in our beds that night.

She sat up, fluffed her pillow and then looked at me with a sly smile. "Do you think you might be in love with Rio?"

"I'm not sure. I hardly know him. And every time I see him I'm doing something really stupid like flashing my undies or falling flat on my face in the sand."

"That doesn't seem to bother him. I think he finds you intriguing."

"So you think he thinks I'm weird?"

Persephone smiled. "Maybe, but in a really cute way."

She lay back down on her pillow and stared at the ceiling fan whirring slowly above us. "Tori says being in love is like a disease. And sometimes it nearly kills you. But I don't know. I've never been in love."

I rolled over on my side and stared at Persephone. "No way."

She shrugged. "I think I'm falling for Jordan, though. When I see him, I get this excited, anxious, sick feeling, all at the same time. Do you know what I mean?"

"Uh-huh." I knew exactly what she meant.

"And you know what I did when you were in the shower?"

I shook my head.

She pulled out a notepad from under her pillow. "I wrote an acrostic poem about him. You know like the ones we did in primary school. The first letter of each line spells Jordan." She opened the notepad, showed me the poem and then read it out loud.

"Jordan is the cutest
Only guy for me
Really like it when we talk

Does something to my heart
And one more thing
No one else is like him."

I smiled. "So sweet."

She handed me the notepad. She had decorated the borders around the poem with flowers and love hearts and then written Jordan's name, probably a hundred times. Yep. She was definitely falling for him.

"You know what I did while *you* were in the shower?" I pulled my sketch pad out from under my pillow. I flipped through the pictures until I got to the most recent one. It was a drawing of Rio on a tiny boat, in a stormy sea. I was flying in to save him on a dragon, not so much because I was into fantasy, but just because I liked drawing dragons.

"Wow! That's amazing! You did all that while I was in the shower?"

"You were in there a long time."

"Still." Persephone stared at the picture a while longer. "I think you're falling for Rio, too."

"You think?" I flipped through the pages of the

sketch pad, revealing the many faces of Rio Sanchez.

"Wow! Look at all those drawings of Rio!"

I nodded. "Guilty as charged."

"You should give him one. He'd really love that."

I shook my head. "No way. Then I'd totally look like a weirdo stalker." I took my sketch pad, closed it and put it back under my pillow.

"Your choice," Persephone said, resting back on her pillow.

"Are you going to give Jordan that poem?" I asked.

Persephone rolled over. "Are you joking? He'd think I was into myself and a total weirdo stalker." She laughed. "I get your point. Some things are best kept between besties."

I felt my heart skip a beat at her calling us "besties." My stupid sprained ankle lie could have ruined things between us, but she'd been really understanding.

I wondered how Mia and Izzy would have dealt with my ankle. I knew they would have been nice to me, but they would have struggled to sit still because I was injured.

"You know," Persephone began, propping herself on her elbow. "We've been coming here for ten years and we've never rented a catamaran. What do you think about sailing tomorrow morning?"

"A catamaran?" I repeated, trying not to get anxious. I seemed to be having an unlucky streak. I sprained my ankle just walking across the rocks. I could only imagine how much trouble I'd get into on a boat.

"Yeah," Persephone said enthusiastically. "Tori never wanted to go sailing, but I think it'd be really cool." She looked at me seriously. "You'd just have to sit on the boat and look pretty. Of course, if you think you're not up to it …"

I didn't know if Persephone threw in Tori's name intentionally or whether it was just coincidental, but it went off like a mini bomb. If I said no to the sailing trip, I'd be just like Tori – no fun at all. And Tori was the last person I wanted to be like. I wanted to be lots of fun, even with a sprained ankle.

"Sounds cool," I said, smiling.

"Really?" Persephone cried. "Even though you've got a sprained ankle, you still want to go?"

"I'm very good at sitting."

"And looking pretty," Persephone added. "And it'll be a lot easier than waterskiing or learning to stand up on a paddleboard."

I laughed. "That's true."

We stayed up half of the night talking more about guys and love and everything in between. We wrote acrostic poems, and I drew a picture of Jordan in a blazing building and Persephone coming to save him on a water-spitting dragon. She tucked that under her pillow with her notebook.

I told Persephone all about Izzy and Mia — and the more I talked about them, the more I missed them and wished that we could all be vacationing together. Persephone couldn't wait to meet them for lunch at the sushi train tomorrow. I was excited too, but I was also nervous. I had to explain my lie to them. I wished I had just told them the truth in the first place, then maybe I wouldn't have a sprained ankle for real!

"I like how they wanted to surprise you about The Lost World. Only besties would do that," Persephone said.

"It was sweet of them," I agreed. "But I'm glad I got to hang out with you, too."

By the time we finally fell asleep, I knew everything about Persephone and she knew all about me. We even had a secret handshake. And I knew I now had three besties.

I was the luckiest girl in the world.

Chapter Twelve

There was a soft breeze blowing the next morning as we strapped ourselves into life jackets at the catamaran rental place. I hobbled down to the water's edge as Persephone, Jordan and Rio dragged the boat across the sand. I was a bit worried about going out with an injured ankle, but then I thought about how cool it was to be going sailing—on our own!

Once the boat was in the water, I climbed on board and waited while the rental guy went through all the instructions about sailing. I didn't listen too carefully because Persephone knew what she was doing.

Captain Persephone had everything sorted out, even the seating arrangements. "Rio, I need you on that side to start off with," she said, pointing to a space beside me. "I'm on the tiller, and Jordan, you can be on the headsail."

"The what?" Jordan asked.

"Sit next to me and I'll explain as we go along," Persephone said, smiling.

When the catamaran rental guy gave us the all clear, Persephone grabbed the tiller thing that steers the boat, and handed Jordan a rope and told him to pull. Seconds later, we were flying over the swells. The beach was fast disappearing behind us, and the cloudless horizon was up ahead. It was just the four of us on the wide blue ocean. It was so exhilarating I almost forgot my ankle completely. All I could think of was Rio, sitting just a few feet away, the wind blowing his hair and the sun on his face.

"This is the life!" Persephone yelled.

I grinned at her and she smiled back. Even in a yellow life jacket, she managed to look cool and cute.

"When did you learn to sail?" I asked.

"I did a two-day course last year," she explained. "I learned all the basics. How to sail, what to do if you capsize and all that. But this is the first time I've actually been sailing since the course."

I smiled. "You make it look easy."

"This part is easy. Here, you have a try. Take the tiller."

I shook my head. "Oh, no. I can't sail."

"Come on," Persephone urged.

The guys watched anxiously as I shuffled over beside Persephone and took control.

"See that headland," she said. "Just aim for it. Pull left to go right and right to go left."

I had a momentary panic working out my right and left. "What if I hit a reef, or a boat? Or a whale?" I asked. I didn't want to put everyone's life in danger if I screwed up.

"Don't worry," Persephone said with a laugh. "Just relax."

I scanned the bay anxiously. There were a few fishing boats, way out farther, and a few guys on surf skis, closer to the beach, but we had clear water all the way to the headland.

"Is it whale season?" I asked.

"Nope, that's winter," Jordan answered.

"What about reefs? Are there any out there?"

Rio shook his head. "We'd see waves if there were any reefs."

"Looks all right then." I took a breath and felt myself relax.

"It really is quite easy," I said a little later when I still hadn't hit anything, or ruined the boat. Maybe my luck was changing.

We all took turns steering the boat as we soared towards the headland. While Persephone ran though some of the finer points of sailing with Jordan, Rio and I lay at the front of the boat. We were on the "tramp," as Persephone called it, which was exactly like a real trampoline, slung from one side of the catamaran to the other. It was perfect for lazing on. We lay side by side, our hands trailing in the water, "like shark bait," according to Jordan.

"You know, I was worried about falling overboard and drowning with my stupid sprained ankle," I told Rio. "I was really nervous about coming out today."

For some reason I thought back to when I first saw The Lads on the beach. I'd been so excited, and they'd turned out to be such losers. Now I felt stupid for even thinking Pit was cute.

Rio was so completely different from those guys. And the way I felt about him was totally different, too. I didn't want to give the feeling a name in case I spoiled it, but I just knew it was really special.

Rio looked at me, and I had to look away and stare at the sea for a moment. He was so cute that I couldn't even look at him. Rio's hand was trailing in the water and I had an overwhelming urge to be closer to him. I watched as my hand moved nearer to his. It was like seeing someone else's hand move, until my fingertips touched his skin and an electric charge ran right through my body. I glanced up at Rio's eyes. It looked like he felt it, too.

"You have nice eyes," he said. "What color would

you say they are?"

"Well, my little sister says they're baby poo," I told him.

Rio's mouth smiled, but his eyes seemed to stay serious. "I think they're sea green." He smiled again and this time his whole face lit up.

And then I knew it. This was what it was like to be in love.

Kitty CHOOSES *Truth*

Chapter Eleven

"Truth," I said loudly, trying to sound confident.

"Truth, hey?" Persephone said, stroking her chin. "Now let me see …"

I giggled nervously.

"C'mon!" Izzy coaxed. "You're killing us here."

Persephone took a big dramatic breath. "So, you're ready to tell the truth, Kitty?"

I nodded, my heart thumping. I'd told enough white lies this vacation. Now I was ready to tell the truth, the whole truth and nothing but the truth. I shot a glance at Rio. He smiled back at me.

"We'll know if you're lying," Persephone warned me.

"Okay," I said, wondering why I ever wanted to play Truth or Dare.

"What's … two plus two?"

Everyone laughed, except me. TC even fell over backwards he thought it was so funny.

"Four?"

Persephone clapped. "Well done," she said. "That was just a practice round. Now for the real question. Are you ready?"

If Persephone was trying to build tension, it was definitely working. I could feel a drop of sweat on my forehead.

I nodded nervously. I was as ready as I was ever going to be.

Persephone opened her mouth when Izzy jumped up and elbowed her aside.

Izzy shined a flashlight in my face. "Tell us the truth. Do you always wear little girls' undies?"

How embarrassing! I glared at Izzy, knowing the only

way to play this was to roll with it.

"Yeah, that's right," I said. "Every day of the week. Monday is Snow White, Tuesday is Dora the Explorer, Wednesday's Rapunzel, Thursday is … Minnie Mouse, Friday is Cinderella and on Saturdays I wear Barbie underpants. On Sundays, I have the day off and wear saggy granny undies."

The whole circle was laughing at me – not really the way I had hoped the game would go.

"Okay, my turn to ask a question," I said, reaching for Izzy's flashlight.

But Persephone got to it first. "Not so fast," she said, grabbing the flashlight. "That wasn't a real question and, Kitty, I don't believe you told the truth."

Mia stood up. "Yeah, that's right! I've seen her in her Dad's leopard-print undies on Sundays."

Oh great! I thought. *Suddenly everyone's a comedian. I'm going to be in the spotlight all night!*

TC really loved Mia's joke. "Good one," he laughed and Mia looked totally pleased with herself.

"We need a *real* truth question for Kitty," Persephone

insisted. She paced around the outside of the circle shining the flashlight on her own face. It was serious, like she was in court about to cross-examine a witness. She was really starting to freak me out. What was Persephone going to ask me that would require such a dramatic buildup?

Maybe she'd ask me about Tori — we had just been talking about her. I wondered if Persephone would ask if I liked her. That would be a totally awkward question to answer. Even though Persephone said I was more fun, Tori was still her friend. And I'd be lying if I said I liked her. Tori was cool and pretty, but she was too much of a princess and a bit on the mean side.

Or maybe Persephone would ask why I told her we were at a rural retreat when we were actually camping. That would make me look like a total liar. It would be bad in front of my friends and really awkward in front of Rio. In fact, any question would be embarrassing in front of Rio. Persephone could ask me something really personal.

I suddenly realized I'd made a big mistake choosing

a truth question. "I've changed my mind. I'll do a dare!"

Persephone looked at me calmly. "Afraid I can't permit that," she said seriously. "I've already decided on my line of questioning." She cleared her throat. "Kitty MacLean," she commanded, "tell us the truth …"

"Uh-huh." I shuffled uncomfortably, accidentally bumping Rio's elbow. He glanced at me and gave me a little nod. Was he trying to reassure me that everything was going to be all right?

"Do you like Rio?"

I gasped. I turned away from Rio to hide my face. For the second time that night, I'd gone bright red.

My mind whirled. No matter how I answered the question I was in trouble. I was either going to embarrass myself with a yes or lie by saying no. And once the answer was out there, I wouldn't be able to bring it back.

I looked around the circle. Everyone had their eyes on me, waiting for a response. It felt like the whole world had stopped to listen.

I couldn't look at Rio, but I felt him squirming

beside me. He must have been mortified, too.

I stared up at Persephone. Did she want to screw things up between Rio and me? Was she punishing me for lying about camping at The Lost World? It was impossible to tell.

Her face became all soft and perfect again. She raised her eyebrows, waiting for a response.

Just as I opened my mouth, I snatched a sideways glance at Rio. He was staring right at me with those gorgeous eyes. In that fraction of a second I knew what my answer had to be.

With my eyes lowered, I replied slowly in a whisper. "Yes."

My whole body tightened. The circle erupted into a ripple of *oh*-ing and *ah*-ing.

When everyone settled down, I felt Rio's shoulder pressing very lightly against mine. I sneaked a peek to make sure I wasn't imagining it. There he was, right beside me.

All of a sudden I understood what Persephone had been doing. She was kick-starting things between Rio and me. She really was very, very cool.

And I was feeling pretty happy with myself, too. I'd made the right decision. Now that the truth was out there, I didn't want to take it back.

I noted the time and the date. This was it. The start of my life.

The End

Kitty CHOOSES Dare

Chapter Eleven

"Dare," I said, hesitantly.

Persephone got to her feet and walked slowly around the outside of the circle, tapping her finger on her lip. Her face was serious, like she was a lawyer in a court or something. It didn't do anything to ease my nerves. She was really putting some thought into my dare. I started to regret my decision.

What if she dares me to kiss Rio? I thought. Of course I wanted to kiss him, but not in front of everyone.

I glanced sideways at Rio. His face looked tense, too. He was probably worried about the same thing. This dare was going to be a disaster!

"I changed my mind. I want truth!"

Persephone looked at me and shook her head. "Afraid I can't permit that. If I'm not mistaken, you called dare."

"Dare!" QC called. Then everyone joined in. "Dare! Dare! Dare!"

I put my hands over my face. My friends had turned into the Rodent Tribe!

"Okay, okay," Persephone said, putting her hand up for silence. Then she took a big deep breath and continued. "I need quiet so I can think."

She started walking around the circle again. "Let me see. What would be an appropriate dare for Kitty?" She made it sound like I was about to be sentenced for murder.

Izzy jumped to her feet and shone her flashlight in Persephone's face. "Okay, time's up." She nudged Persephone out of the way. "I've got one. I dare Kitty to run to the end of the beach shouting 'I love leeches.'" And every ten yards you have to do three jumping jacks and a push-up."

I shot to my feet. I was thrilled that I'd been let off the hook with a classic Izzy dare — more of a workout session than a dare. It would be embarrassing to run around shouting dumb things, but I was sure it was going to be easier than any dare Persephone would have come up with.

Izzy shone the flashlight in my face, shouting like a sports coach. "All the way to the end of the beach. And don't forget the push-ups."

Before I had a chance to go anywhere, Persephone stepped in front of me. "That's not a real dare," she said, putting her hands on her hips. "It doesn't even have a kiss in it."

I knew it was now or never. So I quickly ducked past Persephone, relieved that I'd dodged her dare. She really *had* been thinking of daring me to kiss Rio. What an escape!

"I love leeches!" I said. I then did a few halfhearted jumping jacks and a really pathetic push-up. I had always been bad at those.

"Louder!" Izzy called after me. "And you're meant

to be *running*. If you fail, you'll have to do another dare!"

I picked up the pace. I was sure Persephone wouldn't be so slow to nominate a kissing dare if she got another chance.

As I ran I realized I needed to decide who would go next for Truth or Dare. If I picked Rio and he chose truth, I could ask him anything! I could ask if he'd seen me watching him on the bus every afternoon. But I wouldn't do that, because he'd think I was a total stalker.

I stopped to do jumping jacks and then ran on again, thinking of more truth questions. I could find out Rio's favorite ice cream flavor. That might be a wasted question, but it would be cute to know. I could even ask him if he liked me. I stopped to do a push-up and then decided I couldn't ask that. If he said no, I'd be so embarrassed I'd have to leave the country.

I was almost at the headland, still running through some questions in my mind, when I heard a strange shuffling sound ahead of me. Something big and black was on the beach, digging in the sand. I stopped in my tracks. I was in trouble if it was a feral dog – but it was the wrong shape. After a minute I realized it was actually a turtle, digging a hole, and it was probably about to lay eggs. How cool!

I backed away slowly so I didn't disturb it. Then I turned and ran back to the others. "A turtle! A turtle!" I whispered excitedly.

Izzy was shining me with her flashlight. "You're meant to be shouting 'I love leeches.' And you didn't do any jumping jacks or push-ups on the way back. Looks like you'll be doing another dare."

I waved her complaints away. "No, no," I said, out of breath. "It's really a turtle. Down there on the beach."

"Is it alive?" Mia asked.

I nodded. "I think it's about to lay eggs."

"Wow!" Persephone said, grabbing my hand. "Where?"

We all crept quietly along the beach until I found the turtle again. She'd finished digging and was now laying eggs in the hole.

"Let's stay and watch," TC said.

"As long as we don't go too close, I bet she won't

even notice we're here," Mia said.

Mia directed us into position a few yards from the turtle, and said we should lie on our stomachs so we wouldn't disturb her. As the turtle got on with her mothering duties, Mia filled us in on everything there was to know about turtles. She was quite the expert on them – our very own eco-guide.

It was pretty unreal, lying there on the beach in the dark, watching the turtle lay her eggs and listening to Mia. It also saved me from having to face another dare. On the other hand, my discovery prevented me from asking Rio any important questions. Then I realized that, as Rio was lying right next to me, I could just ask him anyway. I decided to start with an easy question.

"I'd love some mango ice cream right now," I whispered. "How about you?"

"I'd kill for Belgian chocolate."

"Really? I thought you'd be a forest fruit sort of guy."

Rio laughed. "Is that because I remind you of a blueberry? Or am I more of a raspberry?"

"I don't know," I said, smiling. "They're both nice."

I felt my face go red for the second time that night. I was basically telling Rio he was cute with my stupid fruit metaphors. Luckily I was saved by Persephone's phone beeping with a text.

"It's my mum," she whispered loudly. "She's at the campground waiting for me. And we're taking the guys back to Paradise Point, too."

I felt my heart sink. The night was about to come to an end and I hadn't asked Rio anything important.

"Shame we have to go," Persephone said, getting up. "We didn't even get to finish Truth or Dare. I had some really good things planned." She gave me a sly smile.

I felt a shiver run down my spine at the thought of being dared to kiss Rio. I was glad Persephone hadn't dared me to do it in front of everyone. But another time, when Rio and I were all alone, on the beach, under the stars … who knew what might happen? I got goose bumps just thinking about it.

"We should have another round of Truth or Dare," Rio said, getting to his feet. "Next time, you can come to our beach."

"Sure!" I said, way too quickly. I caught Persephone smiling at me again. She knew just what was going through my mind.

"Shame you can't stay a bit longer to watch the nature show," Mia said, not moving from her turtle-watching position. "When she finishes laying the eggs, she'll bury them, then drag herself back into the water. She'll be done in another hour or so."

"Yeah, it's a shame," TC said.

I couldn't tell if he was serious about the turtle or not, but he seemed reluctant to leave Mia. His friend QC was also slow to drag himself away from Izzy.

I stayed with Izzy, Mia and the turtle as Persephone and the guys disappeared into the darkness.

"I feel like something beautiful is just about to begin," I said with a sigh.

"I know, isn't nature wonderful?" Mia said, not taking her eyes off the turtle.

"Yeah," Izzy added, getting nature-loving on me, too.

I smiled to myself. Izzy, Mia and I were talking about two completely different things. I was thinking of Rio, and my friends were obsessed with a turtle.

Izzy and Mia totally rocked, and maybe one day soon Persephone would join our group, too. We could be one big happy gang of four. And, who knew, before vacation was over, we might all have boyfriends! Now, that would really complete the picture. Not even I could draw something as perfect as that!

Kitty CHARGES HER *phone*

Chapter Eleven

I had realized something obvious: *the shooting star didn't matter.* If I wanted anything to happen with Rio, I had to make it happen. I had to contact him.

I raced back to the kitchen as fast as I could.

"Where did you go?" asked Mia.

"I can plug in my phone!" I called excitedly, heading for the kettle.

Izzy looked up briefly from the table, where she and Mia were sorting out candy by flashlight. They didn't seem that interested in my great discovery, but I was as amped up as the stars.

As I plugged in my phone charger I announced, "I'm back on the grid!"

I sat down at the table, watching Mia and Izzy pull out each piece of candy one by one and examine it. I wasn't interested in candy. In a few minutes I should have enough power to check my messages and contact Persephone. At least she'd know I was alive. And then I could think about my next move with Rio.

"And that looks like it's been sat on," Izzy was saying.

I watched as she inspected a green jelly bean. She added it to the largest pile of candy on the table. Mia reviewed a mangled gummy python and then threw it on another pile. "Gross! That one's half eaten!"

"What's up?" I asked, trying to work out their system.

"We're sorting the candy into piles," Mia said. "Half eaten, sat on and okay."

"Which are the okay ones?" I could see only two piles.

Izzy pointed to a bare patch on the table. "That one. Not looking good so far."

Mia emptied her entire candy bag onto the sat-on pile. "They're all squashed."

Izzy picked one up. "I guess they'll still taste the same."

We stared at our squished and mangled loot in silence for a moment, and then cracked up laughing.

It must have been too loud, because right about then we heard rustling outside the door, and then everything happened really fast.

"They're in here!" yelled BB. The kitchen lights flashed on, momentarily blinding us, and seven boys tore into the kitchen, shouting and snatching candy. They disappeared again as fast as they'd come. By the time we'd realized what was happening, it was all over.

Mia blinked in the bright light. "Better than being pelted with jellyfish," she said with a shrug.

A moment later the lights snapped off. From outside the door, a voice called, "Incoming!"

"What the —?"

Splat. Something landed, loud and wet, on the floor right in front of our table.

"Jellyfish!" I screamed. We dived under the table, crouching.

"You're dead, you hear!" Izzy yelled out. Then the

room went silent as we waited for the next attack.

It was around then that I heard my phone beep. It sounded like a foghorn in that dark, quiet kitchen. I scrambled over to grab it. Thirty-four texts from Persephone, and one from an unknown number.

I scrolled through the messages from Persephone:

Where are you?

Where are you?

Where are you? There were a lot of those.

Hope you're OK.

Going home now.

CALL ME!

I texted an apology, briefly explaining that we'd gotten lost, my phone had died, I was sorry and she could text me if she wanted to meet up another time.

I didn't expect to ever hear back from her, but my phone beeped straightaway.

Poor you. See you tomorrow? Stay out of trouble!

I smiled at the message. Persephone was giving me another chance. She was even nicer than I'd thought.

I'd have to work out a plan with Izzy and Mia and

then get back to Persephone. But that would all have to wait. Right now, I needed to find out who had sent me the other text message. Somehow I had a feeling it was Rio.

But what does the message say? I wondered. *Is he annoyed that he waited at the milkshake shop and I never showed up? Or would he say he couldn't stop thinking about me and was coming to The Lost World in ten minutes to see me?* I knew that was unlikely, but it didn't hurt to hope.

"What are you doing?" Izzy asked, shining her flashlight on me. "Who are all those messages from?"

I squinted at her. I felt like a deer caught in the headlights. I couldn't think straight. "I might have a text from Rio."

"And?" Mia asked.

"If it's bad news, it'll spoil everything," I said.

"But what if it's good news?" Mia asked.

"But what if it's not?" I moaned.

I was beginning to regret charging my phone. I should have left it in my bag and kept Rio as a perfect, if imaginary, boyfriend.

Izzy took a few steps towards me and snatched the

phone. "Don't be a rodent. Open the message."

"No!" I squealed, grabbing her arm.

But she'd already opened the message and started reading it aloud. "Hi, Rio here. Hope you're okay —"

"Give it here!" I said, snatching my phone back. I stared at the message.

Hi, Rio here. Hope you're okay. Sorry we didn't see you today. Went for a walk and found a strange picture on the rocks. Was it a message from you?

"No!" I squealed, pressing the phone to my chest. "Oh, no! What have I done? How did he know I drew that picture?"

Izzy grabbed my phone again, and she and Mia read the message. But this time I didn't grab it back.

My head was spinning trying to remember the picture I drew. *It could have been anyone in that drawing. It was just a boy and a girl sharing a milkshake. He couldn't possibly know it was him and me. I didn't write our names. Did I?* No, all it said was "Love." *Love?!* I cringed as it all came back to me. And then I remembered the dragon. That's how he knew it was me. The dragon was just like the one I'd done in class. It was on the picture Rio had rescued from the trash.

"Betrayed by a fire-breathing dragon," I muttered. "Typical!"

"Or rescued," Mia said, raising an eyebrow. "I think you did that picture hoping he would find it."

I gasped. "I did not! Izzy said it would be washed away by the tide."

"What are you going to tell Rio, then?" Mia asked.

"Nothing," I said glumly, grabbing my phone back from Izzy. "I can't reply now because he already thinks I'm a weirdo. If I tell him I did the picture, he'll know for sure I am!"

Mia smiled. "Or maybe he'll think you're a bit kooky, but really cool."

I sighed. I wasn't sure that being "kooky" was far enough away from being weird. I saved Rio's number to my contacts and considered my next move.

"Maybe I could leave him another message on the rocks, this time saying 'just friends,'" I suggested. "And then we could go to the headland tomorrow afternoon and see if he's drawn something for me?" I was just thinking out loud.

Izzy snorted with laughter and then her face went serious. "Who are you? A cave girl?" she said. "Kitty, you've got a phone in your hand. Just use it … or I will."

"You wouldn't," I squealed, backing away.

Izzy took a step towards me.

Oh, man, I realized. *Yes, she would.*

"It's for your own good," Izzy said, snatching at the phone.

I quickly stuffed it into my bra and scurried behind the table.

"Do you like him or not?" Izzy asked, chasing me.

"Of course I like him," I said, hiding behind Mia. "You know I like Rio. He's the cutest guy on the 377 bus. Make that the cutest guy on Earth, probably the whole solar system! But go away, Izzy! I'll text him tomorrow … when I think of what to say."

"Just give me the phone, Kitty," she said, reaching around Mia, "and I'll do it now. Trust me, you're going to thank me tomorrow." Izzy lunged at me and I jumped away squealing.

Mia stopped laughing and held up her finger for silence. "Kitty, your bra is talking!"

Izzy and I froze. I looked down.

"*Kitty*? Kitty, is that you?" It was a guy's voice.

I pulled out my phone, staring at it for a moment and then put it to my ear.

"Hello?"

"Hi, Kitty. It's Rio."

"Oh." My heart was beating so hard I thought it was going to burst out of my chest. "Oh, hi, Rio." I tried to sound normal. "Nice of you to call."

For a second there was nothing.

"Ah, I didn't," Rio said. "You called me. Only, I think it was an accident, because all I could hear was screaming."

I suddenly felt faint and reached at the table for support. Mia guided me into a seat as she and Izzy leaned in, trying to hear the conversation.

"Oh. So that's all you heard? Just screaming?" I said, trying to gulp down the lump in my throat.

"And some other stuff, too," Rio said. "Something

about the 377 bus, I think."

Oh no! I screamed in my head. *Rio heard everything!*

"Hey," Rio's voice came through the phone again. "I loved that picture you did on the rocks. I knew it was yours. I'd know that dragon anywhere."

Mia gave me the double thumbs-up. Izzy was grinning madly.

"Mmm," I muttered. "Me and my dragons, hey?"

There was a long pause, which I mentally filled with plans for my new life on Mars. I knew I would definitely have to move far away after this phone call disaster. I couldn't think of anything to say.

"So, I was thinking," Rio said eventually, "maybe we could meet at the beach sometime?"

I was so shocked and nervous I could hardly string a sentence together. "Are you, ah, sure? I mean, yes. I'd love to." I cringed, hearing myself say the word *love.* "I mean, I'd like that."

"Great," Rio replied. "Persephone said you're at The Lost World. It's a campground, right?"

I panicked for a moment. "Um," I said. "Um, yep.

That's it."

"Thought so. Persephone had this weird idea it was a luxury retreat," said Rio.

"Nope, we're camping," I said, knowing I'd have to come clean with Persephone later.

"All right. Well, I might bring a couple of guys and come down there one day."

"Cool," I said, smiling at Izzy and Mia. They were grinning and punching the air with their fists. I think they were pretty happy to hear that Rio would bring some friends along.

"Oh, yeah," I said. "And bring a ball and we could have a game of volleyball, if you like?"

"Great, and maybe some beach soccer?" Rio suggested. "So, I'll text you when we're coming?"

I ended the call feeling stunned that I might not have to move to Mars after all. Somehow, things seemed to be working out with Rio.

"How cool was that?" Mia cheered, interrupting my thoughts. "Go, Kitty!"

"Rio and his friends are gonna come and hang out

with us," I told them, excitedly.

"We know … we heard. Woo hoo!" Izzy shouted, putting her arm around my shoulders.

Mia bounced up and down. "Must be time for an epic handshake!"

We giggled like crazy as we tapped, slapped and bumped our way through our handshakes. Mia, Izzy and I were too wired to go back to the tent, let alone consider sleep, so we went to sit out under the stars.

As I lay on the grass with my best friends, I was feeling very lucky indeed.

It didn't matter how it had happened, but it had. I was going to see Rio. This really was going to be the best vacation ever.

The End

Kitty DOESN'T CHARGE HER *phone*

Chapter Eleven

I wandered slowly back to the kitchen without my phone. I imagined Rio was walking with me, this time holding my hand. I was glad of the darkness because the stars were impressive, and my fantasy was a lot more convincing without light, too. I stopped outside the kitchen and peered inside.

Mia and Izzy were at the table sorting out candy by flashlight. Mia inspected a mangled gummy python and then threw it on one of the piles of candy on the table. "Gross! That one's half eaten!"

"What's up?" I asked, trying to work out their system.

"We're sorting the candy into piles," Mia said. "Half eaten, sat on and okay to eat."

"Which are the okay ones?" I could see only two piles.

Izzy pointed to a bare patch on the table. "That one. Not looking good so far."

Mia emptied her candy bag into the sat-on pile. "They're all squashed."

Izzy picked one up. "I guess they'll still taste the same."

"Forget the candy and come outside," I said, pulling Mia to her feet. "The stars are amazing."

Izzy grabbed a giant python from the sat-on pile. "Think this one's okay," she said, feeding the snake into her mouth and following us outside.

"See what I mean?" I said, pointing to the stars. "Do you guys know any of the constellations?"

But then a voice came from behind the trees. "They're over here!" It sounded like BB.

Suddenly seven boys were upon us. Two of them tackled me to the ground. "Get off!" I screamed, looking around for Mia and Izzy.

They had been tackled too. Izzy was thrashing to get away, but she couldn't move. Her brothers were on top of her.

BB sat on her chest, shining a flashlight on her face. "Where is the candy? We know you took it."

"Get lost, you rodent!" she screamed.

BB spun around and stuck his butt in her face. "You want me to fire a fart missile? That'll loosen your tongue."

"Do it! Do it!" chanted the other boys.

"Mum!" Izzy screamed. But there was no sign of anyone's mum.

"The candy is in the kitchen!" I shouted, saving Izzy from the missile.

"To the kitchen!" one of the boys screamed. A moment later, I was released. Mia, Izzy and I lay on the ground, stunned. We saw the lights in the kitchen come on and watched the Rodent Tribe tear inside and then run off into the dark with their loot. It was all over in seconds.

I slowly got to my feet, still a little shocked by what had just happened. "You have really disgusting brothers."

Mia laughed.

"What are you laughing at?" Izzy cried.

"Incoming!" called a voice in the darkness.

"What the –?"

Splat. Something landed, loud and wet, on the ground in front of Izzy.

"Jellyfish!" I screamed, ducking behind a tree.

"You're dead, you hear!" Izzy shouted into the darkness.

But by then the boys had run off, probably to go find more jellyfish.

When we were sure the boys weren't coming back, we came out from behind the trees.

Mia looked up to the sky. "Now, what were we talking about before those stupid boys interrupted?"

I sneaked a quick look around the bushes and then finally relaxed. My eyes drifted up and across the sky. "We were looking for constellations. And I can see one. It's the Cat."

Izzy laughed. "There isn't a constellation called the Cat. You're just making that up."

"No, really," I said, pointing to a group of stars.

"There are its ears, and there's a tail."

"And I can see the Tree!" Mia shouted excitedly. "Look, all those stars are like branches, full of beautiful parrots."

Izzy laughed. "I can see Mr. Contra eating a bowl of cabbage soup."

I lay down on the grass to get a better view of the stars. I couldn't see Mr. Contra, but I could pick out someone else's face. "I can see Rio Sanchez."

"Aw," Mia said. "That's so cute. Is Tom up there, too?"

She lay down beside me. "Yes, I can see him. Hello, Tom Cuthbert! Look, he's swimming across the sky to see me."

I looked at Izzy, who was still standing, gazing at the stars. "Can you see someone up there, apart from stinky Mr. Contra?"

She flopped down beside me. "Uh-huh."

"Is it one of the cute campers?"

"Yeah, it's Popeye," she said.

I laughed. "You mean Dan, or Sam?"

"Or Calvin?" giggled Mia.

"Yes," Izzy said. "There he is." She tried to point him out. "It doesn't matter what his name is. I've seen him in the stars!" she said, grinning.

Mia snorted. "Well, it must be destiny then. You'll definitely end up with him."

We all laughed at that. I stared up, looking to see if I could find Rio again, but a cloud had drifted across the night sky. "I think I've lost Rio."

Mia sighed. "Tom's gone, too."

"I can only see Popeye's ear," Izzy sighed. "Ah, well. Easy come, easy go. That's what boyfriends are like."

I smiled. Izzy was hardly an expert on boyfriends. She'd definitely had a lot of love interests, but had never actually dated anyone. She did have a point, though.

"Let's make a pact," I said, lying back down between Mia and Izzy. I took their hands. "Boys might come and go, but besties are forever."

Just as I said that something raced across the sky.

"Shooting star!" we all shouted at once.

None of us were certain that it really was a shooting

star — it might have been another flying jellyfish, or maybe even a jet-propelled set of gummy teeth, or just a plane or a satellite — but I think we all wanted it to be special.

"Make a wish!" I said, clutching my friends' hands and squeezing my eyes shut. This time I didn't wish for a kiss with Rio — I was thinking about Izzy and Mia.

Best friends forever.

One day I might be ready for a real boyfriend. And who knew, maybe it would be Rio. But right now I had everyone I needed.

What more could I wish for?

Kitty STICKS TO THE *plan*

Chapter Thirteen

"I'd like to propose a toast," I said, raising my glass to Persephone's. "To new friends." We clinked glasses.

Izzy and Mia were still busy in the pool taking on the guys at water polo. They weren't helping the Rio situation at all, while Persephone was really looking out for me. She was doing everything she could to make things work between Rio and me.

Persephone and I ran through the whole script again. With George's friends in the pool we had three extra people to manage. But we couldn't make them leave because George might leave with them, and that would make it impossible for the jealousy element to work.

Persephone fiddled with the umbrella in her glass. "You need to do something else to get George's attention. There's too much going on in the pool. He's not going to notice you sitting on your lounge chair."

"What about if I were more like this?" I stood up, flicked my hair and giggled loudly about nothing. Then I pulled my phone out and took a few selfies.

"Wow, that's scarily good," Persephone said, laughing. "You're totally killing it. I almost mistook you for Tori."

I giggled too loudly again. I was getting into this acting thing. "Is anyone noticing me?"

"Oh, yes!" Persephone whispered excitedly. "Here comes George."

I glanced over the top of my phone and saw George and Levi striding towards me. It gave me such a fright I dropped my mobile. I scrambled under my lounge chair to pick it up.

"Now's our chance," Persephone said, jumping to her feet. She smiled at George's friend. "Levi, can I get you a drink?" Then she turned to George. "Why don't you and Kitty sit down?"

I let my eyes drift from my phone to George, who was now standing right beside me. "Hey, Kitty," he said, and then put his arms around me. Before I knew what was happening, he scooped me off the ground. I quickly realized where we were headed.

"No!" I screamed as I was thrown, fully dressed, into the pool.

I resurfaced with my phone still in my hand. A moment later, Persephone landed beside me. Levi had tossed her in.

I clambered out of the pool, dripping wet and mad as anything. I'd saved for a whole year for that phone and now it was as useless as a wet brick.

George was a complete idiot. And I'd seen one too many of them today. That's probably why I walked straight up to him and shouted. "You owe me a new phone!"

"Oh, sorry. Promise I'll buy you a new one." George said, suddenly looked embarrassed. "Suppose you're mad at me for ruining your best shorts, too."

"No, George! They're *my* best shorts!" Persephone shouted, getting out of the pool. She marched over to George. She looked so angry that I thought she was going to punch him, but instead she tripped over the leg of a lounge chair.

"Ow!" Persephone moaned, collapsing on the ground. "I think I've broken my toe."

Levi rushed to help her. "Let me have a look at it," he said. He picked her up and put her on a lounge chair to inspect her injury.

George laughed. "He does one first-aid course and thinks he's a doctor. But it does seem to impress the girls."

Persephone didn't *look* very impressed. I glanced towards the pool to see what everyone else was making of the scene. The water polo game had pretty much been abandoned. George's other friends had gotten out of the pool and were drying off. Mia and Izzy were throwing the ball to each other. Jordan was leaning on the side of the pool watching Persephone and Levi, while Rio floated in the pool ignoring everyone. He dived underwater and I caught him glancing at me when he surfaced, but he seemed more interested in George than me. He probably felt sorry for him. After the way I'd shouted at George, Rio was probably very glad to be well away from me.

Persephone's father wandered across the terrace with his arms full of boxes. "Pizzas are here," he yelled, piling them on the table beside Persephone and Levi. "Everything okay, Percy Pony?"

"Da–ad," she growled. "Don't call me that."

"Sorry. Everything okay, dear, darling, number–one daughter?"

"That's even worse." She glared at her father, but he was already walking off, grinning.

"Anyone for pizza?" George said, opening one of the boxes. A glorious smell of pepperoni, melted cheese and garlic drifted into the air.

"Don't mind if I do," I said, pulling off a piece and stuffing it into my mouth.

The plan had gone so far off course that I figured it didn't really matter what I did now.

After ignoring me all night, Rio chose that exact moment to talk to me. I nearly choked trying to get the pizza down. Then I worked out he had only come over to say good-bye.

"We have to go now. So, see you around." Rio wasn't actually talking directly to me. He was speaking generally to anyone near the pizza table.

"Yeah, thanks for inviting us," Jordan added. He looked at Persephone, who was still sitting down. Levi was helping her to a piece of pizza. "Thanks for inviting us, Persephone."

"I'll show you out," Persephone said, quickly getting to her feet. She'd made a miraculous recovery from her toe injury.

"No need," Jordan said.

He and Rio crossed the terrace and disappeared out the gate.

"Okay, that was weird," Persephone whispered to me. "I think Jordan's got Rio's disease."

I nodded. "Super weird."

Izzy, Mia, Persephone and I decided to get away from the boys for a while. We took the cocktail glasses and other stuff upstairs.

"You and Levi look cute together," Mia said to Persephone, as we loaded the glasses into the dishwasher.

Persephone's head spun around. "Levi?"

"She's into Jordan," I explained.

Mia shrugged. "I thought you must have changed your mind. It looked like you were with Levi."

"You think that's why Jordan looked so annoyed when he left?" Persephone asked.

Izzy nodded. "Pretty likely."

Persephone sighed, and then went over the whole evening in fine detail. "You really think Jordan left because Levi was looking at my toe?"

The three of us nodded at her.

"Oh no way. How did I miss that?" said Persephone.

We wandered off to her bedroom, where mattresses had been made up for Izzy and Mia.

I looked at Izzy. "You haven't quite finished your pizza, Izzy. There's still some on your cheek."

"Thanks." She found a mirror, wiped her face, and then turned to me. "So, are you going to tell me what that was all about?"

"What do you mean?" I said flopping onto my bed.

"I thought you were into Rio and then you're all over George."

"George?" I said, shocked. "I'm *so* not into George. He threw me in the pool so I shouted at him."

Izzy shrugged. "It looked a lot like you were into George. And George is definitely into you. I saw him looking at you earlier."

I gasped. "Our plan *did* work!" I turned to Persephone and we bumped knuckles. "Way to go, girlfriend."

"It's all about careful planning," she said with a grin.

Mia frowned. "I thought you were crazy about Rio."

"Yeah, I am. That's why I pretended I was into George, so Rio would get jealous and –"

"And go home really early with Jordan. Wow! Great plan!" Mia said flatly.

Mia was right. I turned to Persephone. "Didn't really work out so well, did it?"

She shook her head. "Maybe not so much."

Izzy flopped down onto her mattress. "Rio actually seems pretty nice. We spoke a bit in the pool. Shame you screwed things up with him."

"Did he say anything about me?" I asked desperately.

Izzy shook her head.

"Did he say anything about a girlfriend?"

She shook her head again.

"What about cats?" I asked.

"What is this? Twenty questions or something?" Izzy sounded annoyed. "Why didn't you talk to him yourself, instead of blowing kisses at George?"

"I was not!" I protested.

"Wait. One. Minute." Persephone held a finger in the air. "You didn't blow kisses at George, but you *were* blowing kisses at Pit on the beach, right before we met up with Rio and Jordan."

"What?" I said. "But it was one kiss, and I was being sarcastic, remember?"

"I bet Rio didn't notice that."

I rolled over and buried my face in my pillow. So that's why Rio had been acting so weird all day. He didn't have a girlfriend, or hate cats, chocolate or mint ice cream. He must have seen me blowing a kiss to Pit and thought I was serious. He obviously had no idea who Pit was. I was hardly going to be dating a singer from The Lads! And then I remembered the picture of Pit and me. While I was flicking through my photos to find Sid, he probably saw that photo, too. I groaned. "I think he saw a picture of Pit and me on the beach."

Mia frowned. "You showed Rio that to make him jealous?"

"No, of course not," I said. "It was an accident. I was trying to show him a picture of Sid." I lay back on the bed to think. But I didn't get very far because Izzy attacked me with a pillow.

"Hey!" I shouted in surprise. "Izzy, I really don't need that right now, I'm trying to think."

"That's for blowing kisses at Pit." Then she hit me again. "And that's for having a really dumb plan to make Rio jealous."

Persephone piped up. "Actually, it was my dumb plan."

Izzy stared at Persephone and then hit me again with her pillow.

"Hey!"

"And that's for lying about spraining your ankle," Izzy said, whacking me again.

"Okay. I deserve that one."

Izzy turned to Persephone, who was on her phone, texting. Izzy squeezed her pillow and raised it over her head.

"That was a really dumb 'script' you came up with," Izzy told Persephone.

Persephone glanced up from her phone and stared at Izzy, shocked.

Izzy didn't back down, though. She hit Persephone over the head with the pillow. "You really need to chill out more."

Persephone squealed, grabbed her pillow and smacked Izzy over the back.

"Argh!" Izzy cried, like a steel pole, instead of a bundle of feathers, had smashed her.

"You need to grow up," Persephone sneered at Izzy, hitting her again.

Izzy's wail was so dramatic that Persephone's mum came bursting in. "What's going on in here?"

The girls both dropped their pillows and froze.

"Nothing, nothing at all," Persephone said, smiling innocently.

"I don't mind you having fun," her mum said. "Just keep the noise down." She backed out of the room and closed the door behind her.

Persephone glared at Izzy, then looked from Mia to me, a grin spreading across her face. "Pillow fight!"

It was on. And everyone got into it. There was jumping, screaming and whacking. Finally, my arms were too sore to hold up my pillow anymore. I fell back onto my bed, laughing as feathers floated over my head. Izzy and Persephone were still going at each other like it was a fight to the death. Now I knew for sure that they'd get along just fine.

As they kept hitting each other, I was thinking about Rio. I really had to get a message to him. I also had to clear things up with George, straighten out matters with Levi and mend fences with Jordan. What a mess. Our plan had been a total disaster!

"Sorry to interrupt, but I need to borrow a phone.

I have to apologize to Rio."

Persephone gave Izzy one more whack and then turned to me. "Already sent a text."

"What?"

She tossed me her phone. "See if there's a reply." While she was distracted, Izzy got her again. "That's cheating!" She held up her hand. "A truce."

Izzy dropped her pillow and collapsed on the bed. That gave Mia a chance to move in on Izzy. She really pounded her. Then Persephone got stuck in, too. "The password's one, two, two, one," she said between blows.

I quickly punched in the password while the pillow fight went on, and saw the message Persephone had sent Jordan.

Hey Jordan. Think there's been a really big mix up. Can we meet tomorrow to explain? Kitty also wants to talk to Rio. P xxx (Kitty's mobile drowned.)

And then there was a reply from Jordan.

OK. We'll see you at the beach tomorrow. We'll be near the flags around eleven. Jordan

I sat on my bed staring at the message. In just a few

words, Persephone had really sorted things out. She must have done it while Izzy was hitting me with a pillow. Persephone sure knew how to handle stuff. Well, sometimes, anyway.

When the pillow fight ended, we all sat on our beds and I handed Persephone her phone. "Wow, you did it."

"What, what?" Mia asked.

"Persephone's fixed things with Rio and Jordan. We're meeting them tomorrow."

Persephone took her phone and read the message from Jordan. "No, I haven't done anything. You've still got to sort things out tomorrow with Rio and I have some explaining to do to Jordan."

I felt a wave of panic at the thought of meeting Rio on the beach. I'd have to go through the whole story of Pit and Kes, and then explain our stupid plan to use George to make him jealous. It was going to be so painful! And there was no guarantee that Rio wouldn't just walk off. And Jordan might walk off too, because Persephone had been nearly as terrible as I had.

"I better start planning what to say," I said, then I

caught myself (right after Izzy and Mia hit me over the head with their pillows). They were right. A plan was the last thing I needed.

"Actually, maybe I'll just be myself."

Persephone smiled. "I think that's a really cool plan."

Kitty ABANDONS
THE plan

Chapter Thirteen

"Come on," I said to Persephone, stripping off to my bikini. "Let's show those guys how to dive-bomb!"

"Double-decker!" we yelled, hitting our target. We landed right in the middle of the pool with the world's biggest splash.

Izzy paddled over. "I hope you're better at water polo than dive-bombs!" she said, throwing a ball at Persephone, who fired it on to me. I passed back it to Izzy, who shot it to Mia on the other side of the pool.

"Girls against boys!" Mia shouted, firing the ball past George who was in front of one of the makeshift goals. The ball flew past him. Izzy, Mia, Persephone and I all cheered.

It was on. Water polo war. Sure, we were completely outnumbered by the guys, but we had secret weapons: Izzy and Mia. And they were merciless. They pulled the guys under, tossed the ball over their heads and smashed it into the goal. Persephone was pretty good and I did my best, but Izzy and Mia were the queens of the pool.

It was awesome beating the boys, but best of all was hanging out with Rio. I tried not to stare, but it was hard to keep my eyes off him. I loved watching his serious expression when he was chasing down the ball, and then seeing him roar when the guys scored a goal. He was too cute. *Why did he have to have a girlfriend?*

My heart sank when the pizzas arrived and I knew our water polo game would have to end. It had been so fun being in the pool with Rio.

But then, George came up with a new idea. "Let's see what you're like at soccer," he shouted at Izzy.

We all grabbed a piece of pizza and ran onto the beach, ready for a rematch.

Good one, George, I smiled to myself. I liked his plans a lot better than our movie script!

As it turned out, the guys totally outclassed us at soccer. I scored the girls' only goal, but it was only because Rio made an intentional miss. I knew he didn't mean anything by it, but the way he smiled at me as the ball went straight past him made me melt. We could have lost a hundred to one and I would have been happy, because I was having a great time with Rio.

After another swim, there was a final dive-bombing challenge. Finally Rio and Jordan collected their stuff from the lounge chairs. It had been such a fun night, and I hated watching Rio getting ready to go.

Who is this girl who was getting in the way of Rio and me? I wondered. Surely I deserved one chance with him. It just wasn't fair! I wanted to ask him what was going on, but as Rio and Jordan headed off down the beach, all I could manage was a wave.

Persephone sighed as we watched them go. "Jordan is so cute! And he wants to go paddle boarding tomorrow. You up for it? How are things with Rio – any progress?"

I shrugged. "Don't think so."

Just as I said that, Jordan and Rio stopped walking

away. Rio turned and from where I was sitting …

"He blew you a kiss?" said Persephone.

Had I been blown two kisses in one day – one from Pit and now one from Rio? It was too weird.

I felt goose bumps spring up all over my arms. "I guess that's a yes to paddle boarding, then!" I turned and gave Persephone a hug. "He likes me. He likes me!" I sang.

I raced to find Izzy and Mia. They were back in the pool throwing a ball to each other.

"Rio likes me!" I shouted.

Mia swam to the edge of the pool. "What happened?"

"When Rio was walking off he turned and blew me a kiss." I was *so* excited! After a day of wondering whether he had a girlfriend or not, I felt like Rio had presented me with a bunch of roses and a love note.

"How weird," Izzy said. "What guy blows kisses?"

I frowned, annoyed at Izzy spoiling the moment. I figured she was still mad at me for lying about my ankle.

Persephone, Mia, Izzy and I cleared up the remains of the cold pizza and empty glasses and went up to the apartment. While Persephone talked with her parents,

Izzy, Mia and I made ourselves at home in her bedroom. Two extra mattresses had been set up on the floor.

Izzy flopped onto one. "Luxury!"

Mia flopped down on the other mattress. "I can see why you wanted to come here on vacation."

I smiled sheepishly. I still felt bad for lying to my friends about my ankle, but I was glad to be spending the vacation with Persephone. Rio wouldn't have blown a kiss at me if I'd gone camping. But I was so glad that Mia and Izzy were here with me. "Thanks for coming tonight. I knew you'd have fun."

Mia smiled. "We weren't really sure what to expect. But it was actually fun. Did we do a good job of acting?"

I snorted. "A perfect job of acting like yourselves. Persephone and I had other things planned: fruit punch cocktails by the pool, sitting in the lounge chairs, lots of talking, not so much splashing, definitely no ball games and not so much of George and his friends."

"Nah!" Izzy laughed. "The games were the best bit, and George was all right, too. Pretty good actually."

I threw a pillow at Izzy. "Don't let Persephone hear that.

She already thinks people only like her for her brother."

Izzy shrugged. "Is that such a bad reason?" Then she smiled. "Just kidding. She's nice. And much more fun than I thought she'd be."

"So, Kitty," said Mia. "Are you going to try out for the water polo team? You're really good."

"No way," I said. "You two just make me look good."

Izzy sat up on her bed. "You and Persephone should both join. She's got a great right arm."

"And if she's on the team, she'll have to join our group," Mia added.

I loved that Mia came up with the idea by herself.

"She should join our group whether she's on the team or not," Izzy said. "She's way too good for Tori's group. I think I'll suggest it."

"You should," I said, smiling.

At that moment, Persephone walked in, frowning. "I was just thinking that Izzy's right. It was weird for Rio to blow you a kiss. Pit would do that, but not Rio."

"Pit *did* do that, remember?" I said. "So arrogant."

Persephone nodded. "And remember who was right

behind us when you blew the kiss back?"

I groaned. Everything was suddenly making sense. "Rio saw me blowing Pit a kiss!" I gasped. "He wasn't blowing me a real kiss, was he? Rio was mocking me."

Persephone shrugged. "I don't know if he was mocking you, but he might think you're with Pit. Guess Rio doesn't know he's in The Lads and is a total idiot."

I moaned. "Blowing a kiss at Pit, in front of Rio. I'm the idiot!" I said. Then I remembered something worse. "And Rio saw a picture of Pit and me on the beach, too."

Mia frowned. "Why did you show him that? Were you trying to make him mad?"

I shook my head. "I was trying to show him a photo of Sid, but I flicked past other pictures first. He must have seen the photo of Pit and me."

"What are you going to do?" Mia asked, wide-eyed.

I jumped to my feet, suddenly sure what I should have been doing all along. "I've got to talk to him."

I raced out of the bedroom, with my three friends right behind me. Mia was asking a million questions and Izzy was giving me a hard time for blowing kisses at idiots and lying about my ankle. She really wasn't going to give that one up.

"Back soon!" Persephone shouted to her parents as we raced out of the apartment.

We ran down the beach in the direction Jordan and Rio had gone. They were probably long gone by now, but I had to try to find them. I had to explain – not by text, not tomorrow, but right now. Face-to-face. We hadn't gone far when a crowd blocked our way. It looked like a party had spilled out onto the beach.

"They're playing your favorite band," Persephone said to me as we stopped to see what was going on.

Sure enough, I heard the familiar strains of one of The Lads' songs, just over the noise of screaming girls.

"I think Pit and Kes are in the middle of that crowd," I said, peering. I could just make out a couple of guys standing on a mini stage, surrounded by a flimsy barrier and bodyguards. It must have been an impromptu gig. I wondered if we were responsible for that. It wasn't really what we planned with our fan-page post.

"Let's go," Persephone said. "I'm over those guys."

"No, I want to see how bad they are," Mia said.

"Yeah," Izzy said. "Me, too."

"But I have to find Rio." I'd hardly gotten the words out when I saw him. Just up ahead, peering to get a glimpse of the two idiots from The Lads, was Rio.

Persephone spotted Rio, too. "Good luck!"

I walked quickly towards him, my heart brimming with everything I needed to say. I tapped him on the shoulder. *Here goes*, I thought. I just hoped I was right about the mix-up.

"A big fan of The Lads, are you?" I was almost shouting to get over the singing and screaming.

Rio shrugged. "Actually they're better than I thought they'd be. I guess it's the beach atmosphere."

"Did you know The Lads are staying in that building, right there?" I said, pointing at the apartment building.

"Yeah, I heard. We must have walked right past them. That's the ice cream place right over –" Rio stopped mid-sentence. I was sure he had made the connection that I hoped he would. "Are *you* a big fan of The Lads?"

I nodded slowly. "I *was*, but then I found out what

losers they are. They were throwing water bombs at their fans this afternoon."

"But, I thought … Didn't I see you blowing one of those Lads guys a kiss?"

"Ah, yeah, that would be my bad attempt at sarcasm," I said. "We met Pit and Kes on the beach and took some dumb photos with them. They're total morons."

Rio shook his head. "I thought you were … But the photos … You and him …" Rio's voice trailed off.

"You thought I liked *Pit*?" I asked.

"Dumb, huh?"

I groaned. "And *I* thought *you* had a girlfriend."

Rio's face broke into a huge smile and he laughed. "Now that's really dumb, Kitty."

For a few moments we just looked at each other. Rio's face was so serious and cute that I just had to tell him what I was thinking – what I'd been thinking all night and pretty much every other night, for ages.

I was just building up the nerve to tell him I thought we'd make a cute couple when some Lads fans shoved their way past. They were singing and getting right in the way of my important declaration. Then one of them grabbed my arm. I spun around, glaring. It was Izzy! She was singing at the top of her voice, holding on to Mia, who held Persephone, who was clutching Jordan. My friends had joined a conga line and were sweeping around the beach, collecting more bodies.

"Come on," Izzy screamed at me. "It's The Lads!"

Before I had a chance to remind her she hated The Lads, Rio grabbed my waist and we swung off to the sound of "Crazy Girl."

Pit and Kes might have been idiots, but they sure did know how to get a party going. Even Rio was singing "Crazy Girl."

Was he singing it for me, or about me? I wondered.

But really I was having too much fun to care, because Rio's arms were around me. We were together at last!